Contractual Obligations

A.M. Hounchell

Printed in the United States of America

First Printing, 2018

Rusty Wheels Media, LLC.
P.O. Box 1692
Rome, GA 30162

ISBN-13: 978-0692059852
ISBN-10: 0692059857

Printed in the United States of America

Cover Design by Jos. Studios www.josephstudios.net

-Disclaimer- Any resemblance to actual persons, living or dead, events, or locales is entirely coincidental. While some instances or thoughts may appear real, they are merely a perception of reality, brought to life by the writer of this book and the choices you must make.

Dedicated to you. Without you, there is no story.

-A.M.

Special Thanks to Glenn at Sarco Press
www.sarcopress.com

For projects past, and this precious book.
Let there be many more in our future...

-Marc D. Crepeaux, *RWM*

Prologue

Your life had a soundtrack. Not an especially good one like one from a big budget movie, but it was composed from the sounds of your life. It was uniquely yours, and it went into the album you called *Bland*. Whether it was going to be your only album was up for debate, but *Bland* was not going to win a Grammy.

Why would someone want a trophy in the shape of outdated tech anyway? You'd sometimes ponder similar situations. Oh, here's your math trophy in the shape of an abacus. You did a really good job at that English thing, here's your animal skin and your feather. Oh, here's your surgeon trophy in the shape of a bottle of whisky. None of those things made any sense to you as trophy ideas, but you also weren't the head of the trophy decision board.

Your album had four distinct tracks to a slow and boring tempo. Track one was a constant low pitch that was similar to what a printer did when it finished regurgitating digital nothing. It was a precursor to your predetermined destiny, because in the end things played out exactly how they were supposed to, with or without your intervention.

To start the track, you had to force yourself to give eye contact to people who thought they were deserving. No one deserved eye contact, because it is a courtesy, not a right. Still, it was a formality that you went through, because you weren't a crazy weirdo. You did have the capacity to be either *crazy* or a *weirdo*, but not both.

The second track was the simple utterance, "Would you like…" set on indefinite loop. It hardly mattered what was said after the phrase, as long as somewhere in its confines it contained the word *but*. In practice, the music sounded like a robot gurgling gravy, saying something such as, "Would you like to go to a great school, *but* you have to get stupid good grades to do so?"

The third track was the sound of rubber or plastic being opened. It sounded just as much like a doctor opening a glove for a prostate exam as it did a bag of Lucky Charms being opened, but it contained none of the excitement of either.

The last track, though the shortest, was the reminder that the album had a definitive ending. For you, it was like hearing bacon or smelling an ice cream truck jingle; a microgasm for one of your senses. The track was as satisfying as the sound of two quarters being rubbed together while your crush sat on top of a Ms. Pac-Man machine drinking a Coke slushie.

Though the worst aspect of the album was once the

music started playing, you didn't really have a choice but to continue listening to it, 200+ times. You had to listen because you were living it. You were making music to the slow boring beat of your own humdrum-like sequence of off-key tones. You were trapped in the album like a tic-tac in marshmallow fluff or a dinosaur in tar. Perhaps you could run to a better tomorrow, or outrun a bad yesterday, but you were always trapped in the worst of now.

That was the interesting aspect of now. As long as you thought about the future, that's what you were doing in the now. Once the future came around, it would become the now, and the once-then-now became the past.

Until one day, while working at your deathly boring retail job selling shoes or gum or gum-proof shoes or gumshoes, a woman stepped towards your register. She was about to change your tune forever and the tone of your life's story. She was wearing a bright blue blazer and a white blouse. Her shoulder length brown hair was nearly ruined by two cowlicks at either side of her head that made her look especially goat-like.

"Did you find everything alright?" you asked as though you cared. What was she going to say that surprised you? *No, sorry, everything I wanted was suspended above lava and also cursed and made of dry leaves.* You would probably still nod weakly like you did every time, even if she said something so ridiculous.

"Seemed easy enough to me," she said with a roll of her eyes. She set some small items on the counter, and you organized them so that they were all facing upwards. In slow succession, you scanned them all with your strange laser pistol. Her head twisted until it was perpendicular to her shoulder. Though her eyes were firmly planted on your hands, she seemed to be looking through you. At your potential. At your soul. At a box of chocolates set behind you? Who really knew? Obviously, not you.

Taking advantage of her distant look, you decided to ask, "Would you like to sign up for our credit card?"

"No."

"But you would save 10% off if you were approved." This time instead of dignifying your comment with a response, she waved your voice away like an insect. A small insect to be specific. Something like a gnat or a ladybug or an ameba. Is an ameba an insect? Don't know.

You noticed finally that her skin was thoroughly sunburnt, which gave her eyes a sunken look. It had been hard for you as a cashier to tell if people were genuinely weird or just tweaking. Sometimes it was magically both. Those were the people you liked best. Magically weird tweakers were the people who thought you were trying to find their stash of chocolate gold coins via half of their cell phone number. Stranger, the back half of their cell phone number.

You slipped your fingers into the plastic bag and slid her items in with minimum resistance. "Your total is $43.11."

Still quiet, she flipped open her wallet and handed you three crinkled twenties. Then, as she continued to stare through you, she spoke. "I like your soundtrack very much."

If she was talking about your metaphorical soundtrack that didn't actually exist, then she was definitely on drugs. It wasn't like normal people could hear a metaphorical sound. That would be like her hearing your soul, which was, in itself, extra crazy.

She reached back into her wallet, attempting to grab something with her falcon talons. She yanked an old piece of yellowed parchment from the crevice and slammed it onto the counter.

"What is this?"

"A music contract. I want to buy your soundtrack." Definitely a tweaker.

You decided to play along. Honestly what did you have to lose? "But it is boring."

"Perhaps, but I can give you anything for it. *Anything*."

"Stick of peppermint gum?" you asked, holding out your hand. She snapped her finger and a flaming stick of peppermint gum appeared in her hands. She offered it to you, but you pushed her hand back. "No, I just wanted you to chew on that." She narrowed her eyes, but placed the strip of gum into her mouth.

"My powers do not have to be wasted on such trifle jokes."

"What are you trying to get out of this?" you asked the crazy person a question like that. You honestly wished you knew how crazy minds worked.

"I get all of the music you make for a very long time."

You heard rumblings of a fifth track appearing on your album. It was the sound of thunder before a heavy rain. If you took the deal, you could make less *Bland* music. You could do anything. Screw music, you could skydive with your cat!

But was it in your best interest to take the deal? The woman flicked her lips with her forked tongue. You got the impression that she was getting impatient. Your options presented themselves as answers to a multiple-choice question. Each of them were equally possible, probably.

Y OU JUST FINISHED the core of *Contractual Obligations*. It represents a single moment in the main character's life. Like life, there are many options to choose from here. In the end, the only thing that governs life is the next choice. Choose to fight, bake a cake, or even fight a cake.

Life only offers up a single contract, and as a human being, you are obligated to make decisions. From here the story can go in many different directions. Choose any one and see how it plays out. Unlike life though, you can go back, and decide a different path.

All paths are viable, so choose wisely, because choice is now the only thing you have left.

Contents

Choice A

"**A**RE YOU THE Devil?" you asked her, because that was a question people wondered. You are a human. She laughed confidently with the vibration of someone who wasn't.

"No, I'm just a music agent. What gave you the impression that I was the Devil?"

Looking back, you did think it was kind of stupid. Her skin wasn't even that red. It was just a little pink like she had been lightly burned by the sun. "I just had a weird feeling about it is all."

"Well, how about you channel all of that creative energy into a brand-new song." She handed you a pen, and you signed the contract.

In five months, you released a new album called, *The Devil in My Mind*. It became the number one album in the Multi-Verse overnight, and you became the first artist to go Triple Diamond in an hour. You had all the money you could always ask for, and only a shred of memory of what once had been. Your life couldn't be better.

Caviar? You got it. House for your grandma? Why not two? Car for your dog? Not just any car, how about a Lexus? Save the poor orphan children? Save them, but why just give them new houses? Give them all a dog that drives a Lexus *and* caviar for each dashboard.

For one of your albums in your later career, you went back to the shambles of the store where it all began. Even though you had become ridiculously successful, somehow the store that hadn't needed you, was now bankrupt and ruined. You dug through infinite boxes of crap in the dilapidated stockroom, despite the fact that you could've just hired someone to do it (this was an important thing for you, so no one else was going to get the glory), until you found the register that had once been yours. You knew it was yours because it had a chip on the side where it had fallen onto your foot. Remarkably, it still had two dusty quarters in the drawer.

You took it to your enormous penthouse, and you fixed the register one tiny piece at a time. It consumed your days, but you remembered how much you missed your register. In the last song you produced before you retired from the music business, you made sure the last note was the sweet sound of the drawer of your cash register opening. That way you could remind people that from just two quarters, you can become something. 50 Cent made it work, so why not you?

Choice B

YOU WENT TO sign the contract with a nearby pen, but she slapped the pen out of your hand. It fell onto the floor and melted into a pool of vaguely pen colored liquid. You also noted that she had slapped you hard enough that it burned ever so slightly, which was strange.

"Anyone can sign their name or even your name with a pen," she said with a low growl. "I need you to sign with your DNA. Something that is uniquely yours." She handed you a pushpin, and you pricked your finger and signed the contract without question, for some reason.

The ground behind your register began to crack open, revealing hundreds of red figures dancing around a pool of lava. They were chanting your name. You found that you were firmly locked in place despite the desire to leave. The Devil leaned over ever so slightly and pushed you with a single fingernail into the pit.

Even though the fire and flames caked your eyes, you could see your old bland life through the crack. You wanted to go back, but you had signed your life away. Your new album would be titled *Screaming Head with Burning Eyeballs and Flaming Lips: This is NOT a JOKE.* It was mostly filled with music of you screaming in agonizing pain. It did not have an ending. It continued eternally. Interestingly, your torment was just the B-side to several different options. You shouldn't have trusted the Devil, or maybe you should have.

Choice C

YOU SIGNED THE contract, because obviously she wasn't the Devil. Actually, even if there was *the* Devil, what were the odds that she would appear to you? It would be like if the mall you worked at happened to have *the* Santa Claus, which was obviously the plot of some movie with a jerky teen. The kind of teen who rolled their eyes when you told them to have a nice day.

You actually weren't even that religious, so the fact that a thought like that had even crossed your mind was kind of bewildering, but weirder things had crossed your mind before.

You released a new album nearly a year later titled *My Life is a Living Hell.* It turned out that it didn't matter if she wasn't or was the Devil, you were still in your Hell. Which was poetic, sad, and corny like a painting of a fat crying Dorito eating a handful of original people. With all of this money and all of this fame, you had finally accomplished all of your goals and had nothing to strive for anymore.

Your ambitions were impossible to satisfy. You were already a bazillionaire, so everything was boring. You could have used your money for a bank-breaking ad campaign to make people think being broke was the new way to be successful, but it wouldn't have been successful. And even if it was successful, you would never find enough time to burn all of your money to become broke enough to be successful again.

You fell into a deep depression, one that lead to a river of booze and fish made of drugs. You would go to jail a handful of times and eventually have as many DUIs has you did hit songs. You would find yourself actually wishing you could go back to your bland and boring life, but you knew that wasn't really an option. Sometimes at night, you wished that it was possible to meet the real Devil, so that you could actually get into really real Hell.

There wasn't even an option to stop producing music, because you were contractually obligated to release a record every two years for the rest of your life. The night you died of a drug overdose, you dreamt of quarters being rubbed together. For at least a moment, you were happy, and in that moment, you died. It was a sad turn of events.

In death, that ridiculous dream to meet the real Devil would be fulfilled. With an open hand, she would welcome you to Hell, and it was a refreshing change of pace. In Hell, you got to play in a demonized version of St. Peter's band, *Heaven's Haven* called *Heaven's Heathens*. Lucifer was your lead drummer, and you were the lead singer, so it wasn't too bad.

Choice D

"YOU ARE OBVIOUSLY the Devil," you said matter-of-factly.

"What is your point exactly? Was I not explicit?" The Devil said as she smiled. It did seem particularly explicit after you looked closer.

"I'm obviously not going to sign that. You are trying to take my soul."

The Devil let out a long pained sigh. "It isn't like that." She rolled up the contract and placed it back in her purse. "I don't really want your soul."

"Then why did you try to make me sign my soul away," you screamed, ignoring the gazes of the customers in line.

The Devil placed her head into her hands. "I need your help okay? I can't find anyone who will help me!"

"I doubt that you actually need my help. I'm a person and you are like a fallen angel. What would you want with me?"

She slammed her fist into the counter leaving scorch

marks in the shape of a flipper. "Some kid beat me in a fiddle playing contest, and I lost my golden fiddle. I want it back!"

"You expect me to believe that some kid beat you in a fiddle playing contest? That sounds like the most ridiculous thing I've ever heard. Did you get that from a country-themed box of cereal? Or just the theme of a big-box country-themed song for cereal? What was her name?" You were not convinced at all. You had been led to believe that the Devil was a trickster and would do anything to get your soul, but she did seem genuinely distraught.

"His name is Johnny."

"A kid named Johnny beat you in a fiddle playing contest? How did he even do that? Don't you have some ability to sense how good someone is at the fiddle at least? Or some demonic power to make his wrist cramp? Literally *any* powers?"

Now, even the people in line were convinced she was the Devil. They were also convinced that she sucked at being the Devil.

"He said he was the best that's ever been. I didn't believe him, so I jumped to conclusions and a hickory stump too quickly. And for your information, I wasted my demonic power on a band of demons. They sounded something like this!" She punched the counter again, leaving a flame on the counter that danced like three demons playing backup fiddles. "Sabotaging him would have made more sense. Damn him all to Hell!"

You never thought you'd think this, but you felt

genuinely bad for the Devil. You agreed to help her under the condition that she didn't take your soul, but you didn't make a physical deal. Instead, you both fist bumped, because it seemed less binding. A paper trail was not something you wanted tying you to the Devil.

She taught you how to play the fiddle well, and you became very good and even impressed with your ability to learn. At the end of your extensive six-month training, you wandered through the forest. The Devil had said, "Look for a young man playing the fiddle hot." When you finally found him, playing a golden fiddle, you jumped up on a hickory stump.

"You play a pretty good fiddle boy, but give it back dude. I want your fiddle of gold, because I know I'm better than you," you said.

You were going to verse Johnny for the golden fiddle. Luckily, a golden fiddle sounded like garbage, so it didn't matter that you choked. You took the fiddle back to the Devil, and you felt good about your deed.

She ended up giving you a real music contract, no strings attached, which was nice of her. Although it turned out later that *no strings attached* was a clause about the instruments, which had no strings. This was also okay, because plenty of instruments don't have strings. All in all, everything turned out moderately fine.

Choice E

INFINITE OPTIONS EXISTED as long as you never answered. Most tests were like that, if you really thought about tests. It was strange that tests have time limits, because nothing changed if it took you longer to figure out that one answer. Once you had the woman pegged as the Devil, for example, but then as you looked up, you realized what you had thought was red skin was actually a red suit. What you had thought was the point of horns was actually a red cap with a fuzzy white ball on the end. How had you been so wrong? It was almost as if some unknown force had pushed you to deduce that the woman in front of you was the Devil, when she was in fact Santa Claus.

"So, do you want the contract? It's a good opportunity," Santa said.

You pricked your finger with the pin and signed the contract, because who wouldn't want to work for Santa. Besides Krampus, but Krampus was a cramp. You had just made a deal with jolly Saint Nick for some reason. He smiled at you, and you shook hands over the deal.

Approximately thirty days later, you found yourself on a stage, getting ready to sing an interesting version of Jingle Bells. Santa had you practice this version of the song every night since you signed the contract, meaning you had it down to a mechanical level.

"Welcome to Santos Mall! I'm one of Santa's elves, and I will be performing *Jingle Bells* in the language of Christmas!" You opened your mouth and everyone began to cheer before you made any sound.

Everything and everyone were looking perfect, and you had the feeling that you were about to gain a new notch in your CD. Figuratively, because a new notch in your physical CD would make it so it didn't work. It was more like an extra track on your belt. Somehow that didn't seem right either. "Longa sals. Longa sals. Longa la de ra! Vo want sa ez tor law..." You started to realize that everyone was staring up at you, but not normally like when people stared at a movie. That's right, you have been staring at movies you weirdo. Instead with unblinking eyes, they mouthed your lyrics. They were hypnotized by your incredible singing. You continued to sing, and the people chanted along with you, until you realized that they were actually hypnotized.

Santa appeared with a laugh, "Ho! Ho! Ho! Now, stand up and rise against the greedy children of this world and kill them all!"

"What are you doing?" you asked. "You are supposed to be a good guy."

"I'm eliminating the evil of the world, what else could be *more good*?" The people of the mall pulled out candy cane guns and marched into the world. Now, you kind of wished you had made a personal deal with the Devil instead.

"That isn't a good solution!" you screamed, but Santa brushed it off.

"It is however, a solution nonetheless." You watched as the thousands of people wandered into the world looking for the bad kids.

"Wouldn't it make more sense to help the bad kids be good instead?" you asked.

As you turned to look at Santa, he was brandishing a candy cane gun with the festive level set to max. That was enough to turn your organs into gumdrops.

"That would be much easier, but I've been working on that for hundreds of years. Are you with me or against me?" Santa asked, pulling the Twizzler on his gun ever so slowly. "I urge you to really think your choice all the way through."

You wanted to say something, but mere hesitation made Santa shake his head. He took a shot, and you gum dropped to the ground. "Why?" All you wanted was the opportunity to make a different choice.

"Kids are evil and by comparison, I am good." Santa stepped over your body, and he continued into the world with his candy cane raised in the air. Who knew how many children were going to be destroyed by the ideas of Santa. Not you, because you are dead.

Choice F

YOU COULD EASILY take the music deal right then and there, but something inside your gut told you that this particular deal wasn't about the music. Whatever the Devil was up to, it was just a front. There was no way in Hell (or out) that she would actually want your music. Unless she was going for an ironic take on what she wanted for Hell's Elevator music; like a 'bore them to death' kind of situation. Which would be weird since it would be double the death, thus defeat the founding principle of Hell in general, but perhaps there was something like Double Hell with a catchy name like *DubHell*.

"You don't want the deal?" she asked you, pushing the tempting contract closer. You went to read more of it, but unfortunately, she pulled it back. "You cannot read the fine print when you make deals with the Devil." What she didn't know was that most people didn't read fine print anyway.

"How can I trust you?" you asked.

"Easy. You can't. That's the beauty of it. You don't know exactly what you are getting into. It's like a Christmas party, where we exchange gifts. In both situations, it can end in a living nightmare. What do you say? Want to try a Devilishly good Christmas party?" She slid the contract closer to you again, careful not to reveal too many of the words written in small type on the paper.

What exactly could you lose though? You were already a cashier. And you already had lame music that played all the time in your head, along with actual lame music that played on the million-year-old speakers overhead. Really, all you could get out of this deal with the Devil was some entertainment. You pricked your finger, and a single drop of blood rolled off of your finger towards the parchment. Once it hit the paper, it was accompanied by a thunderous boom. Your reality quickly tinted red around you.

Once you regained your composure, you found yourself drinking from a glass filled with dark red punch. You savored the carbonated cherry taste until the last drop, and then you set the glass onto nearby table. It seemed as though now, based on the decorations alone, that you were at a literal Christmas party. This begged the question, since you could no longer hear your *Bland* album, if you had merely created the situation in your head out of pure boredom.

A woman ran past you carrying a battery powered radio. "The new Christmas song is on the radio!" She screamed excitedly. Everyone in the room flocked towards the radio.

The radio crackled on and you could hear yourself singing to the melody of *Bland* and everyone in the room was going bananas. It dawned on you quickly that Devil had given you fame as far as you could tell, but at the same time, she had removed your consciousness and put it into another body. So even though you were technically widely successful, you had to enjoy it from the sidelines.

Suddenly, you realized the music had stopped playing and everyone was looking at you. Not just looking, they were staring. Could they hear your lack of music accompaniment? Their personal music began to shift to the sound of fire crackling, and magically they were all carrying torches. This was the worst day of your life.

"You is the person who made a deal with the Devil. Kill 'em!" The mad, mad mob chased you through the mad, mad world. This wasn't what you had expected. As you ran through the backdoor of the building, you found that you had been inside of a building marked with your face.

Actually, every single building in the surrounding area had your face on it. The sky had your face on it. The ground had your face on it. You ran, but no matter how fast you ran, you were always watching yourself. It was a terrible dystopian future that was run by you, but not for you. It had only been entertaining for a few moments. Now, you knew that it wasn't a good idea to make deals with the Devil.

You just wished that you could double down on your soul, and get another opportunity.

Choice G

COULD YOU MAKE a deal with the Devil? Probably not. You physically could, sure, but it still seemed outside of the spectrum of things you were willing to do to rebel against the machine. It was also vaguely against the things you were willing to suspend your disbelief to try. Though the contract was sitting right in front of you, you still decided to push it back to her. "I'm against this."

"Are you sure?" The Devil asked with a flame-licked smile.

"I'm 100% sure," You said back. The people in your line clapped and cheered you on. The walls fell away, leaving you standing on a register set in a much larger hanger.

Sitting in a chair holding a megaphone, there was another version of you. The version of you winked, and then vanished into shimmering dust. "Cut!" someone yelled. A short man waddled towards you with a cigar in one corner of his mouth and a sucker in the other corner. You honestly weren't even sure if he was super mature for a baby or very childish for a full-grown adult.

"See, yar `spose ta take de deal. It's sorta the whole pointa dealin' wit the Devil. Wer makin'a movie, so itsa portant dat we catch ya choosing ah deal." Then he flicked his fingers, and the walls leapt back into position. "Ya got it? Make dae dal." The man smiled.

With one hand, he pointed a shiny gem into your face, and you instantly forgot what had transpired. What was it again? You rubbed your eyes, trying to get your composure. You vaguely heard someone breathing in front of you.

"Ahem," you heard someone cough. Once you regained your sight, you saw that the Devil was standing before you. She was offering you a familiar, but enticing contract. Could you make a deal with the Devil? Probably not. Well, you literally could, but it was against what you were willing to do to rebel against the machine.

"I'm against this," you said to the Devil.

"Are you sure?" she asked

"I'm 100% sure," you said.

"I strongly suggest that you take the deal," the Devil said as she pushed the contract back to you with a shaky hand.

You shook your head, and in one final glance, you caught a glare from a silver colored gem. It hit you square in the chest, and you began to burn away. "This one is defective," someone said.

"Jus bring me another an set it all upa gain," the

director baby-man said. "Ya know that they won't let'us stop 'til we finish da scene correctly." The short manly baby looked up at the distant window, and he saw the outline of a monster that made him turn back to his set.

Choice H

YOU REALIZED THAT the woman in front of you couldn't be the Devil. That was impossible. Plus, you had made a New Year's resolution not to believe in mythical creatures anymore. If you did not believe in them, they were not real. You had chased enough future dream memories of a unicorn for the last time through the woods. That same future dream memory had been the first time that you had ever seen a lumberjack.

"I don't believe in you," you said clearly. She smiled at you, grabbed you by the collar, and held you above the counter.

"You think I'm a mythological character, do you? I'm as real as they come. I will be back for you in seven days. Exactly seven. Seven." The Devil vanished in a wisp of blue smoke.

After a near deal with the Devil, your boss allowed you to go home early. They all saw the Devil vanish right in front of you too.

Day 1: You found that you couldn't sleep. It was hard to tell what was real, and what was a mythological character. On the way home, you thought you saw the Big Bad Wolf, but it could have been a dog with hallucinated armor. As you were lying in your bed, you thought you saw the Devil run across the hall and into your closet. You were also sure that there was a peanut butter goblin in the cabinet that you kept your peanut butter in, brandishing a knife on a regular basis that was stained with the ghostly remnants of last year's lunch. He said things like, "You are what you eat."

Day 2: You slept this whole day, trying hard not to peek above the covers. You could hear the Devil and/or the peanut butter goblin klickkliacking in the hall. Something that was easy enough to avoid as long as you couldn't see it.

Day 3: The Devil was sitting at the edge of your bed watching you. She kept licking flames on her lips. It was as if she was looking through you and into your soul. It made you consider if you even had one. You were starting to notice that another track was appearing on your album, and this one was mostly creepy background music to a strange 70s Halloween movie.

Day 4: You now locked yourself in a closet. The Devil had been scratching at the door, and she was whistling at you. The song that she was whistling was clearly *Honkey Tonk Badonkadonk* by Trace Adkins, but completely off-key, making it seem like Jingle Bells instead. Regardless, she whistled it while walking past your door and running her talons across the wall.

Day 5: Now, you were unsure whether the song was

by Trace Adkins. Was that song sung by George Lopez? Did George Lopez sing country music? At any time at all? Now, you weren't sure whether or not you knew who George Lopez was. The Devil was still clawing at the door whistling that same tune. Jingle Donadonk by George Adkins.

Day 6: You found a George Lopez CD in the closet, but now you don't have a CD player. Also, you were still worried about the Devil. She seemed angry. Maybe it was possible that she didn't know who sang that song either.

"Hey, can you get me a CD player?" you asked the Devil.

"Would you trade your soul for that CD player?" the Devil asked. That sounded like a fair trade. You didn't really need a soul, at least you thought you didn't. It was important to figure out who Groovy Lopez was.

"Sure," you said. The Devil slid the contract under the door, and you placed a hair on the signature line.

The room burst into flames and the door gave up on being a door, and it turned into its true self: a pile of ashes. The Devil was outside holding your CD player. She handed it to you and bellowed into laughter. You slammed the CD into it, and then you realized who George Lopez was. He was that peanut on the side of Sixty Minute Ready Whip Maid Lumber's trucks. You still didn't really know who he was, even after listening to the CD.

Day 7: You spent this day in hell, which was really nice. It could have easily been Miami slathered in lava gravy.

Choice I

THE DEAL WITH the Devil was still on the table for you. You could hardly imagine what it was like to make a deal with the Devil. You know that since you had never really seen her before, except for that one time at the County Fair. Yet, as you looked closer at the parchment, you noticed that it wasn't a deal at all. What you had thought was a deal with the Devil was a recipe for *The Devil's Devil Food Cake*.

"What do you need me for?" you asked the Devil. Fair assessment, because you had never been very good at cooking. Every time you made toast, you had found that you would just rip the bread when you spread the butter over it. It still tasted okay when you put it into scrambled eggs. Sort of the bread, butter, and eggs of your life.

"I need you to harvest some souls to complete my Devil's food cake recipe, so that I can enter a baking contest," The Devil said to you with a smile. She seemed genuinely interested in being in a baking contest, but you didn't really understand why.

"Who's holding this contest?" you asked the Devil.

"No one other than Death himself. I want to get on Death's good side."

"Why?" you asked the Devil.

"Because Death has Michael's angel food cake recipe, and I want it, so that I can sabotage it, and prove that my cake is better. No one has said that food is *angelishly* good, but they do say that it is devilishly good."

"Isn't that because that wouldn't grammatically make sense? Wouldn't it make sense for them to say something was *heavenly*?"

"Cents, sense, since. Tomato, potato. Honda, Toyota. Godzilla, Betty White. They are all just words," she said, moving her hands about like an insane person.

You look closely at the recipe, and you see that one of the ingredients is the soul of man who died in a lumberjack's uniform, which isn't especially sinister, but it did seem oddly specific, but as stated before, you didn't know how to cook. You didn't know the culinary benefits of death in lumberjack uniform. You actually didn't know if that was a normal ingredient for normal food. It probably wasn't, but you had no actual idea. Lumberjack death could have been a key ingredient in chicken cordon bleu. "Why can't you do it?"

"I cannot physically take souls without them being offered to me, but I can give you the power to do it. It is a loophole." The Devil handed you a red glove with long sharp talons. "Once you find a lumberjack, take his soul and I will use it in my cake. Deal?"

It did sound better than your stupid retail job, but so did things like being tied to a log heading towards a saw, because at least saws didn't have reasons to be a jerk to you. A saw was just a saw. It never saw a reason not to be a saw. It never ceased being a saw. If you saw it, all you would see was a saw. Saws were really the perfect friend, because they never judged you. They always split the check, and when they made a fuss, you got into the movies for free.

Regardless, you looked right at the Devil and said, "I'll take your bet, but you're gonna regret, because I'm the best that's ever been."

"Couldn't stop yourself, huh?"

"Didn't know if I would ever see you again." She gave a hesitant nod and shrugged.

Later, you found yourself, just kind of chillin' in the woods, hanging out in a tree, waiting for a lumberjack to just sort of stumble through.

What you hadn't thought was that being a lumberjack wasn't really a popular profession anymore. As a matter of fact, it was possible that no one was a lumberjack anymore. As far as you knew and saw, no one had ever been a lumberjack, ever. You had seen them in movies, but you had also seen dragons in movies, and you were pretty they didn't exist either. It could easily have been an imaginary job like a telegraph delivery person. Or lumberjack/telegraphy delivery person.

As you sat there at the top most branch of the tree, you contemplated briefly whether or not there was a lumberjack named Jack, who had started the whole lumberjack thing by cutting lumber and being named Jack. That would probably piss Jack off. Maybe you'd ask if he preferred Lumber or Jack, or Lumberer Jack. It didn't really matter, you didn't know jack.

Then before you knew it, you thought you heard someone stumbling through the trees, which was what you had been waiting for. The sound of twigs breaking was the easiest sound in the world to identify, because it sounded like being snuck up on by an axe killer, even when it was just a rabbit. It was like music to your ears. You wondered if this particular lumberjack had the sound of an ax guitar playing in his sound track, or the sounds of an ax being sharpened, or twigs snapping in his album. Maybe his album was called *Got Wood? Wood You Axe Me a Question?*

Then you saw it, the plaid red and black shirt, the long brown beard, and the bright red end of an ax. All you needed was to take that man's soul, so that you could make a really delicious cake to steal a cake recipe from the archangel Michael. This was definitely better than work as a cashier. You jumped down from the tree and landed with a thud on the forest floor.

"Here to steal my soul?" The lumberjack rolled his eyes.

"How did you know?" you asked.

"The Devil has been hunting lumberjacks to extinction, so that she can make her famous cake. I'm the last lumberjack in existence. When I die, there won't be any more lumberjacks ever again. Be careful as you approach, because this ax is really sharp." The lumberjack swung his ax, and it split a tree near your head. "See what I mean?"

You were starting to wonder if the Devil just didn't want to take the lumberjack on just because he was dangerous.

The lumberjack swung his ax again, but you caught the handle with your non gloved hand. You had learned the move while catching candles that had fallen from your register. Then with your other hand, you grabbed the lumberjack's soul through his stomach. It was a slippery green thing, but it was easy to pull out like a loose thread in a sweater.

"That's too bad," you said. You didn't really care. Would killing the last lumberjack in the world haunt you at night? No. It was like eating the last spicy mustard pretzel. Yeah, it was kind of a bummer, but it didn't really affect anyone.

You snapped your fingers and the Devil appeared. She looked happy once she saw the soul squirming in your hands like a hairless green cat.

"Give me the soul!" The Devil yelled, but she had a twinge in her voice like she wasn't going to use the soul for a cake. You could hear the sound of triumphant trumpets playing from the Devil's head. She was tricking you, which made sense, because she was the definition of evil. How did you ever think she was being sincere?

"Why?"

"That was our deal, wasn't it?"

"What's the soul add to your cake?" you asked.

"It preserves the freshness!" The Devil yelled.

"Why couldn't you just use sodium benzoate?"

"Give me the soul or I will kill you."

"They were hunting you, weren't they?" You just realized your terrible mistake. You moved closer to the lumberjack, but the Devil lifted the shimmering red-tipped ax.

"Choose carefully! As he said, this ax is sharp!" she growled.

You moved closer, and the Devil swung the ax. You slid under the ax, and you placed the soul back inside the lumberjack. You were able to save him, but the Devil was already swinging the ax at you. Taking that deal was going to be the death of you very soon. Like, just now. (You are dead.)

Choice J

"YOU HONESTLY DON'T think that I've never been warned about this? There's like a thousand country songs about the Devil, comic books, operas, and countless short stories! You are in the freakin' Bible being a jerk and the Bible is in like every single room in existence on a statistical average. What makes you think that I will take this deal?"

That's right. You just told off the Devil. You've had to deal with your crappy boss long enough that no amount of the Devil's shenanigans was going to make you crack. You worked retail, you dealt with customers. Those were people who were entitled. The Devil was nothing in comparison.

"Don't you have something that you really want, more than anything? I can offer you any amount of things for your music." The Devil pushed the contract towards you, but you instinctively tore it in half. Almost magically, the contract reappeared in your hands, except there were now two of them. Cut one head off, two contracts regrow.

"Yeah. My soul is worth more than a wish that you are going to botch. It's like making a deal with a genie, except I lose any chance of going to heaven." You tore the contract in half again, and you threw it into the trash.

"I get such a bad rep from an old book. I'm actually really cool. I thought that apple would be delicious. I'm not that evil." The Devil said as she put on a set of stunner shades.

You scoffed. "Yeah right. I don't buy it. Can you hurry up? There's other people in line." The Devil slid her card over to you.

"After work, you can come over to *Hell 'N 'A Hand Basket* and hang out." The Devil left with a sad look on her face, but you didn't really care.

But in sixty hours when your shift was almost over, you'd been worn down enough to actually go hang out with the Devil. It beat working or being alone in your apartment. Plus, she was like the only person/demon that you knew who would be awake and not busy at 8:00pm in your town.

You showed up to *Hell 'N 'A Handbasket*, and you were pleasantly surprised to see that it was an ice cream parlor. The Devil was behind the counter, wearing a surprising amount of mint chocolate chip ice cream. "You work here?" you asked.

"I don't just work here. I own this ice cream parlor. Pretty cool, huh?" The Devil picked up a warm scoop and swiveled it around in her hand. "Want a scoop or two?"

You looked at the ice cream flavors. *Soul berry, Forbidden Fruit Punch, Chocolate Chip Cookie Dough, Vanilla Mean, The Dark Side Fudge, Devil's Food Cake.*

"Can I get some Devil's Food Cake?" You ask.

"You read that wrong. It's the Devil's Devil's Food cake. It's my own special recipe." The Devil dipped up a scoop of chocolate-y ice cream into a waffle cone and held it out for you. As you took it, you could have sworn the Devil smiled. She actually seemed pretty cool.

As you moved the ice cream towards your mouth, there was a flash of light. Suddenly, there were two Devils. One brandishing an ice cream scoop, and another one wielding a lumberjack's ax. You recognized such an ancient artifact from the history channel. Aliens were always using them to pry open Egyptian doors so that they could steal dusty vases for their dusty vase museums.

Without a second thought, the ax Devil sliced off your hand that was holding the ice cream. As you fell to the ground, bleeding out, you watched as the "ax Devil" put her ax, blade first into the "ice cream Devil's" chest. Too bad. You got one lick into the ice cream, then death.

Special K

As you were looking at the contract, you had that strange revelation that you have every 13,457 seconds exactly. Sometimes, you woke in a cold sweat with the realization. It was the same revelation that was pulsing through your body in this moment.

Nothing was real. Nothing had ever been real. You were merely the side effect of some crazed alien ruler who had been binging on blue bean dust which was mixed into clear jelly. This episode with the Devil was like all the others.

"So, do you want the contract or not?" The Devil asked again. Sure, she was speaking, but you couldn't hear her. This idea. This concept. It was nothing. You could feel all the various pathways that life could have given.

What if you had said yes to little Susie Waterson for a glass of lemonade? What if you had rolled around that toxic waste? What if you had two thumbs on one hand but none on the other? What if Oreos were a hard drug? What if you knew the answer to every what if?

You were having an existential crisis, because you always had them. They were merely every four hours. Every four hours the concept of time dissipated, and you were subject to contemplating the existence of your life.

"Do you want it or not?" she asked, but slow and fast, hot and blue, and cold and green.

Everything you had ever known was a lie. There were no people named Johnson. Because there had never been any people. Why would people get upset when you say their name wrong? It isn't like they were born with that name. No one was born with a name, because no one had ever been born. You weren't even sure if you had ever been real.

The world around you spiraled away in the great flush of the cosmic toilet. As everything shifted back into its correct position, you found yourself in the true universe. You were a lizard inside of an ice cube. You were melting in the sand of a beach made of crushed pomegranates. The sky above you was made of a large red beach ball, which smelled like a warped surfboard. This was what everything was supposed to be.

The moment in which everything had been estranged from its original concept stopped, and you were left again with the choice. You were now looking at the Devil. You were looking through her eyes and into her brain. Nothing was and nothing ever would be. This meant there was no reason to take the deal, because anything she could produce for you would never be legitimate. It wasn't like the Devil could just magically send you to a separate universe with its own unique events.

At the same time, it meant that there was no reason not to take the deal, because there couldn't be consequence. If nothing was, then there was nothing to fear, but fear itself. You could ask for anything, but you would never have to deal with consequence, because consequences were subject to the rules of existence. Where you were in the world, there were no rules. Perhaps, if you inhaled more, you would float right into the ceiling. At least then, finally, you could change the light that was out above you.

This was how it was going to be forever and never, because it already happened. You were going to be looking at the Devil, contemplating your answer, and nothing would change. Nothing could change, because you were the one thing that had existed, and you needed to move before everything else could. Reality was perpetual and based on your movement. This moment was where you were trapped, in a dead-stare with the Devil, locking yourself in that now and then.

Choice L

"DEAL OR NO deal?" The Devil asked with a smirk. She slid the contract off the counter and set a briefcase where it had been. The people standing in line lifted another set of cases each with a different letter burned into the side. Some of the cases were still smoking from being branded. You just realized that you were on a gameshow. Not just *a* game show, you were on *the* game show of the millennium. Emphasis changes everything. You were on *Wheeling and Dealing Devil*. How had you never noticed before? In Japan? It was so clear. You weren't a cashier. That had been a facade the entire time. This was just how every episode of the show opened.

"All you have to do is pick a case. You have a chance at winning back your soul! One of the cases has an even better soul inside of it! This week's sponsored soul comes from Attila the Hun, because he doesn't need a *t* to hun*t* you down. Are you ready to play Wheeling and Dealing Devil?" You were so excited. This was the first time that you had ever been on a gameshow.

"I'll take the 666 case." An older lady from the cashier line moved up to the register and handed you the silvery case.

"You picked the 666 case, so you get to spin the WHEEL of UNFORTUNE! Do you know how this works?" The Devil asked you. You nodded your head excitedly. "Then spin the wheel!"

You grabbed the wheel and spun it around. Shrunken head. Knife covered in blood. Blood Star. $10,000. Shrunken head with a blood star! The wheel stopped spinning, and it landed on blood star. "I can't believe this!" you screamed.

"It's time for the Round of Judgement! All you have to do is pick from three sets of two people, and decided which of the set had the largest amount of evil inside them. It is as easy as knowing what is right and what is left." The Devil gestured to a screen behind you that you didn't remember being there. You had a bad memory.

The first set of pictures was Hitler and Betty White. "You can't really think this is difficult?" you asked.

"Remember that if you get one of them wrong, you have to fight Cerebos in the *Eternal Pit of Flame*," the Devil said. The studio audience cooed at the idea. No one ever won a fight against Cerebos.

"Hitler, obviously!" The pictures flashed green and moved onto another set of pictures. The next set was of Cleopatra and Alexander the Great. That was an actual tough choice. You looked at both pictures. "Cleopatra!" you screamed. The pictures flashed green again and moved onto the next set.

The last set was two pictures of you. That was interesting. One of them seemed to be a live feed of you looking at the pictures right that instant, and the other picture looked like you wearing a shiny glove while holding a weird, slimy, green ghost. "What is this?" You asked as you turned to the Devil.

"These are two versions of you. One of them is eviler than the other. Pick one," The Devil said with a Devilish smile.

"There are two versions of me?" you asked.

"There are many versions of every person and thing, including me. This is but one world of many. Pick carefully."

You looked at the two pictures. You were inclined to believe that you weren't the eviler of your two versions, but you weren't actually sure. "The other one is the evil one."

The Devil laughed. "Indeed he is. What were the odds? Now, solve the puzzle on the side of the briefcase, and you *could* win *your* soul back."

There was a puzzle cube on one end of the briefcase in place of a lock combination, which looked impossible to solve.

"If you are unable to solve the puzzle in 60 seconds, then we take you straight to Hell! Go."

You saw that the case had an almost unperceivable etching of the horrified faces of what you thought to be its victims. You slid the puzzle one direction, and what was once a cubic puzzle turned into a triangular puzzle.

You contained your breath and slid the puzzle around again, revealing a keyhole behind the rectangular puzzle. You pulled off the rectangular portion of the puzzle, and it morphed into a key.

Just as the last precious seconds were ticking away, you pressed the key into the hole.

"Congratulations! You just unlocked one of your souls! Now, I'm going to take your current one." The Devil opened her toothy mouth and sucked your soul into her gut. As the light flickered away from your soul, the soul from within the briefcase moved into your body. Initially, you came back online, streaming. You felt different, but you were still the same. Like the same recipe made by two different people.

You were happy to see that you weren't about to be killed by an ax. At the very least, that was nice. You did not want to be killed by an ax, because that was very low on your list of preferred ways to die.

"Now, you can pick a door! Any door! Choose carefully again."

"Where am I?" you asked.

"Where aren't you? Pick a door." The Devil smiled at you.

"This game doesn't actually have an end, does it?"

"I don't know. Does it?" The Devil asked, her head tilting impossibly to one side.

It took you too long, but you had finally realized that you had been in Hell the entire time. How hadn't you noticed?

Choice M

YOUR MUSIC WAS hard to hear, but you knew to stay tune to yourself. You shouldn't take deals with the Devil. Lots of artists thought that it was socially acceptable to make deals with the Devil, but you were above doing things like that. You weren't Vincent Van Gogh, or Snoop Dogg, or Mike Birbiglia. Plus, it was clearly inside the employee handbook. Right under the fact that you were required to wear pants at work.

"No thank you." The Devil left unexpectedly without saying another thing, and you realized how easy it was to get rid of the Devil. It was a simple, the just say no policy. The next lady in line came up. She was an older lady, but she seemed rather nice. She smelled like butterscotch and looked like she might be named Rhonda.

"I can't believe you turned down the Devil so easily. You must have divine gifts. I work for the Great Otherworldly Deity, or G.O.D. as you know him. If you feel so inclined, you should come to our base of operations."

The lady didn't buy anything, and you were left to do your job, no longer bothered by crazy people who wanted your music. Instead, you were left to be bothered by people who wanted pants for 50% off for no reason other than they asked.

Eighty-seven hours later, after your shift ended, you found yourself back at your apartment, still listening to your crappy album, wishing just a tiny bit that you had taken the Devil's offer. You realized that no matter what, it would probably end badly for you. You were lying in your bed, daydreaming about the future, when you got the hankering for chocolate milk. You jumped from your bed and made your way to your fridge. With a sudden click, you opened it, and a heavenly light poured out from the inside of the fridge. What initially took the shape of a fridge seemed to have morphed into a small pearly gate.

"Come to us," an angelic choir sung to you.

"I just wanted some goddamn chocolate milk." It always seemed like important things were stopping you from drinking delicious chocolate milk.

You moved through the fridge, careful not to knock the pudding onto the floor of your apartment. You ascended a flight of glowing white stairs until you were standing in front of a blue door with angel wings etched into it, trying to catch your breath. The older lady from your job, garbed in gold and white armor, opened the door and gestured for you to enter.

You entered a planning room with a hologram of the Devil in the center of the table. There were a couple of other people in the room who were wearing similar armor as the older woman.

"You've seen the Devil in the flesh," she said.

"You were there," you said simply.

"But you were able to disregard the Devil's charm, which seems to be a complete impossibility for a mortal. This means that you are either partially a demon or you are partially an angel. Or some otherworldly creature, like Keanu Reeves."

"So?"

"So, *you* can kill the Devil with powers that are that strong!" Another person moved over to you, she gestured with a tongue dispenser for you to open your mouth. Another armor wearing person grabbed your hand, pricked it, and gathered your DNA into a tiny shred of paper.

"When are you going to know?"

The older woman moved towards a large computer as the other armor wearing angels placed both samples of your DNA into a canister in the back of it. It whirled and spun, causing your saliva and blood to mix together. The results came up on the screen. 0% angel. 0% demon.

"This is impossible," the older woman said. She stroked her chin and considered for a second. "Run a secondary creature scan."

The results appeared rather slowly on the screen. 0% unicorn. 0% leprechaun. 0% centaur. 50% lumberjack.

"I thought all of the lumberjacks were killed off by the Devil."

"Lumberjacks aren't mythological..." You said.

"Jack cut down a beanstalk to kill a giant. A lumberjack saved Little Red Riding Hood and her grandma from a wolf. Lumberjacks are the *only* heroes of myth. A lumberjack is the only person that can stop the Devil with the holy ax."

"You are kidding, right?" you asked.

"Have you ever met your father?"

"No, but that is hardly the point."

"Your father must be the last lumberjack in existence. That is truly amazing," the woman said.

You rolled your eyes. "Where is this holy ax? What is it, in a holy block of wood? Probably in a holy forest? Next to a holy block of cheese?"

"It isn't in this version of reality. We will have to warn other versions of ourselves with music," the woman said.

"You can't be serious."

"I'm never not serious."

"I am starting to realize that."

"Realization is something mere humans cannot quite grasp ahold of," the angel Rhonda said.

"How are we going to 'send music' to other versions of ourselves?" you asked, glancing vaguely in the direction of a blinking light. It was blood red with tiny black horns. *Was that the Devil?* you wondered.

"*We* will not be sending music to *us*. Instead, we will be sending it to a different version *you*." Rhonda moved towards a CD switching tray. A CD popped out towards her, and she grabbed it. Branded directly in the top was a single letter. **M.** "It seems as though the CD Tray of Absolute Destiny thinks that we are on the M rotation of the multiverse. The Devil must have started her universe breaking interaction with you twelve universes ago. If she continues to burn through all of the disks, then everything could be destroyed."

As Rhonda continued to talk, you slowly slunk away towards the door. She was crazy, and you were pretty sure that you were crazy too, considering you were inside of your fridge.

"Where are you going?" Rhonda asked.

"To eat my sandwich that was in my normal fridge." You wandered away, outside of your fridge, and once you opened it again, it was a normal fridge. You took your sandwich, you ate it, and you never saw the angels or the Devil again.

Choice N

THE DEVIL SEEMED pretty serious, and despite the fact that you had heard plenty of bad things about the Devil, she had never actually done anything bad to you. You were the kind of person that judged others based on how they treated you, so who exactly were *you* to say no to someone who never wronged you, even if they wronged humanity as a whole?

"K," you said confidently. You pricked your finger, and you signed the contract, without hesitation.

"You are about to be a star!" A blinding white light consumed your soul, and you could feel your bodiless essence being pulled through the floor. As you passed through the bottom of the floor, you watched as a bright red horned soul passed by. That soul smashed into your body, and then the physical 'you' was gone.

You passed through hundreds of layers of ground until you finally started to sink into an orange and red cavern filled with lava, fire, and brimstone. This must be Hell. An iron chain clasped around your leg, and a pickaxe formed in your hand. Before you was a nine-foot-tall demon with a whip.

"Mine or die!" he screamed.

You lifted the pickaxe, but it was wrapped in barbed wire and extremely heavy, so you dropped it. The searing pain in your palms was hard to ignore, but you were going to have to do it eventually. Once you finally got it raised, you swung it at a nearby rock, causing the rock to scream and bleed out small rubies.

"I'm not already dead?" You swung at the screaming rock, and it began to bleed even larger rubies.

"You wish you were dead."

So, you continued to swing your pickaxe at the screaming rock. Your hands became bloody themselves because the barbed wire cut your skin every time the pickaxe made contact with the rock. Time didn't seem to flow naturally, and you weren't even sure how long you had been in Hell, despite your watch saying it had been two minutes. Your watch had lied to you before.

Once there was a pile of blood rubies, a small demon with a sack made of human flesh came by and collected them.

"30 second break time," the demon screamed.

He tossed you a bottle of what you could only describe as salt water or sweat. You drank it and sat near the rock, not really caring what the liquid was.

"Pssst! Hey pickaxe swingin' bloody hands," someone said. You looked around, but you didn't see anyone but the huge demon. "Stupid. Look down here." You glanced down, and you saw that the ruby rock had a face formed into it. It didn't really look like a human face, more like a cat's face. If a cat was made of creepy red jelly and had been through a blender, maybe. "Behind me is a good ax shaped guitar. If you grab it, you can kill the demon, and you can get out of here. If you do, you have to come back for me."

You weren't exactly sure why the screaming rock was helping you, but as you peeked around the edge of the rock, you saw the ax guitar on the other side.

"Break time is over!" The demon whipped you, and you continued to hit the screaming rocks with your pickaxe, causing it to bleed more rubies.

You were waiting for just the right moment to spring forward and grab the guitar, but the hard end of the whip was intimidating you. If the demon hit you with the whip, you were afraid that it would easily kill you.

With a sudden pain biting you in the butt, you swung the pickaxe as hard as you possibly could, causing the rock to scream louder than it ever had. Then you acted as though the pickaxe was stuck in the rock.

"What in the Hell is going on?" the demon yelled.

"The pickaxe is stuck." The demon moved over and put the whip on his belt. As he reached over to grab the pickaxe, you grabbed the ax guitar and swung it down hard on the demon. Instead of killing him, as you were initially told by the rock, it just dazed the demon for a mere second. He grabbed the guitar and slung it into the distance.

"That wasn't a good idea," the demon grabbed you by the throat and crushed you into a similar rock to the one you had been hitting with the pickaxe.

"You were supposed to play the guitar! What made you think to hit him? The point was to strike him down with music," the rock said.

"It just seemed to be the right thing to do, like, I had heard about it from someone else," you said.

Now, you were doomed to be a rock in Hell. You should have just played that ax guitar rather than trying to beat a demon senseless with it.

Choice O

THE DEVIL'S OFFER still stood. Actually, even the Devil still stood still. This wasn't the first time that the Devil had tried to buy your playlist off you. It was actually kind of sad that the Devil couldn't remember who you were. Despite the fact that she wanted your personal music, she didn't seem to remember that she had wanted it before. It was like how a baby forgot about a shiny object that you had just dangled in its face right after you took it away. The fancy people called that concept *object permanence*.

"I'd rather not."

"But anything in your wildest dreams could come true," the Devil said with a laugh.

"I prefer getting what I want the old-fashioned way," you said.

"What's older than making deals with the Devil?" she asked.

"Deals with Sun Gods, or Greek Gods, or Greek Sun Gods, or Sons of Greek Sun Gods," you listed.

"You will regret this," the Devil warned.

"I doubt that I will."

In a huff, the Devil threw fire at your register, which you calmly put out with a moist towelette. "Have a great day."

Then just like that, the Devil was gone. Your boss was pretty understanding when you asked to go home. She didn't really want to deal with the Devil either.

On the way back, driving in your crappy car, you saw a garage sale.

It took all of thirty seconds to convince yourself that you needed to stop there. As you stepped from the car, you saw that this particular garage sale was selling the typical garage sale stuff. Baby clothes, romance novels, miscellaneous glassware, and crappy PS2 games with someone's initials carved into the top with a sharpie. Then you saw something behind a yellow coat that interested you. It was a skateboard.

"How much for the skateboard?" you asked.

"It's not for sale."

"Not even for this much." you handed the guy a crumpled twenty dollar bill. His eyes lit up as though he thought that you had wanted the skateboard for a measly dollar.

"I've conversed with my good pal Andy Jackson, and you can have it." You shook hands with the guy, and you grabbed the skateboard. As you moved towards your car, you saw one of Hell's Gargoyles land atop a house across the street.

"Not this again."

The gargoyle threw a ball of fire at your car and upon touching the metal exterior, it caused your car to explode. The hellish thing of the night looked toward you and another ball of fire appeared in his hand. Automatically, you hopped onto the skateboard and began moving down the hill that seemed to continue sloping forever.

The gargoyle flew directly behind you, throwing fireballs in your general direction. For the most part, they seemed to land to the left and to the right, but sometimes, they landed directly in the middle of the road. As you were skating down the hill, you noticed a shimmering neon bolt of lightning hovering above the road. Reflexively, you grabbed the lightning bolt, causing your body to glow a brilliant yellow. As the yellow energy consumed you, you began to speed up. Finally, you saw the end of the hill, and you thought that you might get away.

However, as you approached the bottom of the hill, the gargoyle threw an extra-large and extra-powerful fireball that opened the ground up to reveal Hell. Now, you were falling into a bottomless pit. Presumably, it lead to the bottom of Hell.

The gargoyle was diving at you, but for the most part, you could easily dodge him. Every once in a while, there was a spike that jutted from the wall that you had to dodge. Then, as you continued to fall into hell, you got struck in the back by a fireball, causing you to lose your last breath and die.

In front of you in huge white letters was: GAME

OVER. Then in smaller letters were the words: Insert 1 Coin to Continue.

As the timer ticked down to zero, you heard the Devil laugh, followed by her saying, "I told you that you would regret it."

And just like every other life you lost, you did have regrets, like the gargoyle had said. If only you could have sold your soul to the Devil for fifty cents.

Choice P

T HE DEVIL HAD been waiting for your response. You weren't really sure what you wanted from her or from having your own music accompany you everywhere. They both just happened. But as you glanced up, she seemed impatient, and you did not want to make the Devil angry. She was already red enough.

"I'm not really interested," you said casually, which was probably a mistake.

Before the Devil could respond, a flaming pentagram appeared on the ground beside her. A column of flames towered from it, burning your eyebrows off, but only your eyebrows. As the flames subsided, there was another version of the Devil standing there, DubDevil. With her clawed hand, she cut the other Devil's face wide open, making her Deadevil.

"Are you in all these worlds?" the living Devil asked. She crouched down to scoop up some blood, and she pushed it into her mouth. This caused a strange set of runes to appear on her face. The runes were bright blue set into her cherry red skin. Another pentagram burned into the ground, causing another pillar of fire to explode into the ceiling.

"Good riddance," she said as she clawed you in the neck.

Briefly, you felt the warmth of your blood going down both your neck and throat, and time felt blurry. You fell forward, unable to catch your breath. The Dubdevil vanished into wispy smoke, and another version of you appeared, glancing down at you just before disappearing again. This was the last thing you saw before everything went black. It was as if you were asleep inside of hot lava, while having ice water dumped on your head.

Your vision began to come back on, and you were aware that you could not move. You were strapped to a chair with iron rope. There was a woman with wings and a flannel shirt standing in front of you, smiling. If you would have guessed her name, you probably would have said Susan, but that would have been wrong. Her name was clearly something like Rhonda.

"You are going to be okay." You looked to your arms, and you saw that they were gone. They had since been replaced with axes.

"What am I…" But you never finished your sentence, as it seemed right just the way it is.

"We wanted to know if you could handle the ax handle, but we got a little bit too scientific," she said as she flicked the ax that was your left arm. "Now, you will have to handle everything with an ax handle."

"How…" This sentence didn't end either. Could you finish sentences anymore, because if you couldn't, it was going to be terribl...

"Don't worry, you are gonna sleep forever now." She covered your face, and you felt your head become fuzzy, and then you were gone.

Choice Q

THE DEVIL WAS offering you a chance of a lifetime. Maybe even all of the lifetimes. A deal with the Devil could get you out of this crappy job and take you somewhere meaningful. You went to sign the contract, but the Devil grabbed your hand, and she snickered. "Look to that old woman and say, I just got bamboozled by Satan's sister Vil De."

It was just that moment that you realized you were on a game show. Vil De was a lesser Demon who traveled across the land offering people deals that she couldn't even produce, because she had crappy dark magic. Instead, as you remembered it, she would force someone to say her name, and then she would gain an extra boost of power momentarily.

"No," you said.

Vil De frowned. "Why not?"

"Because I have to get back to my job."

"Wouldn't you rather be on my YouTube channel? It'll be in the top ten."

"Nah," you answered. Once you turned back towards your register, you heard the faint click of your *Bland* Tape being flipped over to the B side. As it began playing, it opened with a soft acoustic guitar, then it slowly crescendoed into a heavy electric guitar. A bright red portal with an impossibly one-pointed star appeared on the ground, summoning a huge frightful version of the Devil, covered in blue runes, and with glowing black eyes.

"Hey sis," Vil De said. The Devil slowly moved her giant hand towards Vil De, and she wrapped just her index finger and thumb around Vil De's throat. It took only a second for Vil De's face to go from bright red to purple. Then the terrifying Devil grabbed one of the customer's and popped his head off and drank his blood like a Kool Aid Jammer.

You had a scanner, which was similar to the shape of a gun. If guns were in the shape of something that was completely useless, but you really needed to come up with something, this was it. You couldn't run either, because the Devil was standing between you and the door. You lined up the scanner, and you flashed a red beam into the Devil's eyes, causing her just enough discomfort to drop Vil De.

"Vil De! Vil De! Vil De!" you screamed. The three times you said her name combined into one huge version. "VIL DE!" The clutch phrase wrapped around her in flaming red armor, and the final piece of the puzzle was a giant pair of scissors that appeared from the V in her name.

"Why are you doing this?" Vil De asked.

"Because I can," the Devil hissed back.

You took their conversation as an opportunity to clamber away, but the Devil had melted the door to the floor. The distant rock music in your mind switched to the next track, which sounded like the lonely harmonica. It was the kind of song you would hear if a character in a western was by himself, playing around a campfire.

The Devil grabbed the pair of scissors, and thrust them into Vil De's chest.

"I'm too powerful for you to destroy," she said.

"Vil De! Vil De!"

But it was too late. The Devil's lesser sister fell headfirst onto the floor, and you were sitting on a duck. It wasn't a real duck, but rather a plaster duck made of smaller ducks in a duck-shaped trench coat.

"I see you there," the Devil said, starting to move towards you like creeping magma.

You realized that you had the power to change any situation by changing your music. You did everything in your power to imagine a battle theme, but for some reason, the only thing you could imagine was the theme to the Powerpuff Girls. Despite this, you couldn't get it to manifest on your track. No matter how much you concentrated, you couldn't hear the music.

The Devil took a seat. "You are trying so hard," she growled. As she sat there, she held up a tape, which clearly had Bland written across it with a permanent marker. "Looking to change this, I assume?"

"How did you get that?"

"You sold it to me in some other reality. It's music to my ears, since this whole traveling to alternate realities keeps bringing me back to you. You go ahead though. Try to make something else appear, and then I'll kill you. Close your eyes and try."

Even though you didn't trust her, you didn't really have anything to lose, so you closed your eyes.

"Surprise!" The Devil slashed you across the chest, and you started to bleed, probably to death.

"Wha?"

"Gotcha." She licked the blood off of her talons. "As if I would let you think of something. What did I look like? An angel?"

Yet, as you felt the warm blood pulse through the slash in your chest. You realized two things: Slash played a guitar. And guitars sometimes came in ax shapes. The tape in the Devil's hand morphed into a CD, and the permanent marker turned into Dis Track.

"A dis track is the best you can do? I'm quivering in my goat hooves." She threw the CD across the building, and it spiraled back onto one of her talons and began playing as it spun.

"La la la la la la la la lalalalalala doo dooo dee doo deedada doo de dad," the track played. It was your voice and it sounded just as bad as you thought it was going to. "You… call yourself the Devil, because… that's pretty much your name. Or is it a ti-tal. What's the difference if you want to be called by it. Call her Shelby, she'll throw a fit. Call her the Dark One, and Lucifer may throw a fit. She won't stand for it, why not sit. Call her Devil, or you'll forget. Because those aren't her name. Even if you call her that, it won't be the same." Your music was odd and disjointed, but it was enough to keep her listening. You moved effortlessly away from the Devil, and you began to whisper into Vil De's ear.

"Vil De. Vil De. Vil De. Vil De." The Devil's sister gained enough strength to stand on wobbly legs, and she struck the Devil across the face hard enough to send her through the window of their lives. Where she went, nobody knows.

As Vil De lost her strength, and she collapsed to her knees, you made your way to her. Before you could say anything, six winged people appeared from a swirling vortex that looked similar to a CD. They grabbed Vil De by her collar and pulled her back through the opening of the giant portal.

"You!" One of the winged people yelled. She had a name tag across her shirt that read as Rhonda.

"Have we met?"

"In another time and in another place. Do you know anything about the Ax Guitar of Hell?" she asked.

"No."

"Then you are of no use to us in this realm." Rhonda held up her hand and the distant Dis Track flew into her hand. "I'm taking this."

They left you standing there, partially wondering what your boss would think, also wondering what you thought had happened. You needed a whisky or a doctor.

Choice R

YOU FELT AS if you could take the deal from the Devil, but something seemed to be stopping you. You were completely unable to move, and suddenly you realized that no entity was moving, not even the Devil. A strange green diamond had appeared above your head, and you felt like someone was watching you.

"Kevin, I don't really like the idea of a deal with the Devil. So, change it," an eternal voice said.

Everything blinked, becoming nothingness, and then the scene around you began to change. Everything changed like an Etch-a-Sketch being shaken as hard as possible. It blurred the lines that had been drawn and written previously, creating something entirely different.

Now, you seemed to have a name. It had become your story. "I could see", you would say, if you had a say, which you did not. You could only act through the will of the green diamond above your head.

The world began to crumble around you,

accompanied by the sound of paper crunching. Then, you were dead. You were gone. You were trash, because you didn't have enough promise. Except you had the core ideal correct. You were a good idea, even if you never actually had good ideas yourself.

You had the idea that you could take the deal with the Devil, because you can always do things. There are no laws or rules. There are only suggestions. One topping only at the ice cream parlor? More like as many toppings as you want, because there aren't any ice cream topping police. If there was such a thing, you could probably shame them out of giving you a ticket.

"You said that this was a deal for my soundtrack?"

"No. I am actually more interested in buying the rights to your life, so that I can write a book, because even though previously I said I was the Devil, I am actually William Shakespeare. I want to turn your story into a novel. America's first great novel. I'll call it, *Contractual Obligations*."

As illogical as it was, it was hard for you not to see that who you previously thought was the Devil was actually William Shakespeare.

"Kevin, you are getting soft. Changing the Devil to William Shakespeare is not only unoriginal, it doesn't change the plot at all. I think you may have lost your edge of this story," the eternal voicemail said.

The same crumpling paper sound happened, thus destroying everything you knew. Perhaps you did have promise, but you were circling the metal colored black hole of reality.

You could take the deal with the Devil, but you were secretly an angel cop. You were three months from being a detective. As soon as she made it very clear that she was the actual Devil, you were going to arrest them.

"What is this? This deal was already struck. You are running out of juice. I wish there was more for the story, but this isn't it," the cosmic voicemail said. You winced, realizing everything around you was about to crumble. Then just like that, reality was crushed, and you were killed. "Try again or quit, Kevin."

You were facing the Devil, right after she offered you a deal. She wanted to buy your metaphorical soundtrack, which you could still hear in the background on your life.

"I want your deal," you said. You cut your hand open and dripped blood onto the contract. The piece of paper took on an amber luster as your blood pooled. Even the Devil, bringer of darkness and evil, was slightly surprised by your actions.

"And what would you like?" the Devil asked. She pulled the blood drenched contract away from you.

"Juice. I want juice. I want to pump up my life."

The Devil nodded, "I think I know what you want." Using yellow energy, she created a sphere of blue light. "This will give you that juice you need. Don't misuse it." She tossed the sphere over to you. As it passed over the counter, your soul ripped itself from your body, and floated across the counter in the opposite direction.

You were about to lose your soul for a ball. A ball for

your soul. It was not a fair trade, especially given the fact that once the Devil had your soul, she was going to kill you. It was going to be the last looped portion of your track. The Devil opened her clawed hand, and your soul touched it, but it was ripped away from her. Standing nearby, a lumberjack was using gloves to draw your soul to him.

"Who are you?" the Devil hissed.

"The last Lumberjack in the multiverse." He grabbed your soul out of the air, and contained it in a bag with a goldfish.

"You can't be Lumberjack Jack. You're the guy who saved Little Red Riding Hood from the Big Bad Wolf," the Devil stated.

"Yes. And you are the Devil. Satan. Lucifer. You are the one who forced humans to live this lie. The bringer of destruction and death," Lumberjack Jack said.

The Devil twisted her body towards Jack and let out a smidge of a chortle with a hint of sparks. "I resent that Jack. You know the destroyer of worlds better than me, and you know that it isn't me." A whip materialized in the Devil's hand, dripping with magic. "If I hit you with this, you will die."

"You don't want to kill me!" Jack yelled. Effortlessly, he glided over to the emergency box. It was the same emergency box that was set inside of each of the "stores". This one was an emergency *Hit Really Hard With Your Fist If the Devil Appears* box. Jack punched the box, and an axe popped from the top like a piece of toast. He snatched it from the air and readied himself to swing it.

"You know this isn't going to end well for you," the Devil said.

While the two of them contemplated fighting each other to the death, you were trapped, staring at your own hands. Without a soul, nothing really felt like it had meaning. Sure, you could take breathes, but to what end? Sure, you could stare directly at your arm, but what will your arm say when it notices? Probably nothing. Do arms talk? Would they ever talk? What would they say if you could hear them talking? Lift this! Lift that! Rawr, I'm an arm!

Your senses clicked in such a way that you realized you were holding an orb. Or maybe it was a ball. What was the difference? Levels of important? The ball of life? Basketorb? You tossed the orball into the air and you watched as it sparkled and shimmered like it had a background made of a Lumberjack and the Devil clearly fighting to the death.

The orb fell back into your hand and it exploded in a spectacular display of blue cosmic energy. The blue wave knocked the Devil and Jack onto their backs. Your track gained a pop song. It had a quick upbeat tempo, but a very low bass sound.

"When the bodies hit the ground. Will it make a sound. If you are all dead. What is left. What is right. Can I feel the difference between day and night if I am blind. Blind to the witness and blind to the judge. Wish that I could ever understand love." You threw the orball into the air again, and it shimmered even brighter. This time,

it was orange. It was orange like a fiery lemon consumed by hatred.

It fell back to the ground, touching your hand again. This time it caused a tidal wave with the energy equivalent of a lava pulse. It smashed into the Devil and it smashed into Jack, forcing them both to their knees.

"What is that thing?" Jack screamed towards the Devil.

She winced as another colored wave passed over her body. This time it was toxic green with the consistency of sludge. "It is a bouncy ball. It has no use. I don't know what is happening."

Jack moved just right, so that your soul was under his feet, and his axe was above it. As he brought it down, he sliced the soul in half. Surprisingly, it didn't change you or anything.

"Why didn't that kill you?" Jack screamed. Even as he panicked, he was formulating a plan. Pinch of terror. Once of courage.

"Because," you said with your new, deep echoing voice, "I work in retail. I never had a soul." You clasped your hands around the orball, its glowing energy expanded around your hands like a fire. "Now, if you'll excuse me, I have a universe to demolish." The energy from the orball consumed your body, destroying both your psyche and your resolve.

Once you fully formed the ball of energy, it had a simple skull shape as it passed from your hand towards the Devil. With every bit of her strength, she ripped the fabric of reality and teleported away. The skull of fire and flames ripped through the storefront and continued melting to the horizon.

"I guess she left you to die, Jack," you said. You rotated your hand in the air, and the flaming skull of death rotated around.

Jack knew in that movement that there was nothing he was going to do. "Please, if you can hear my God, help me," Jack said. His face shifted to confusion briefly, then he placed his hands together, "Please," he said again.

"God can't hear you here!" you screamed. The fiery skull gained momentum.

Just as the fiery energy ball was about to strike Jack, a portal opened directly behind him, and the Devil pulled him through. Jack fell onto the ground on the other side of the portal, and the Devil smiled down at him.

"I wasn't about to let you die over there. You are the only being who can stop the power of that orb." she said.

Jack looked around, and he could see that they were in a field of sunflowers and bunnies. "Where are we?"

"I shifted us one reality to the right. We are safe here for the time being." The blue light from your orball of power smashed through the ozone of the new reality and burned the ground.

"How is this possible?" Jack asked, slinging the ax over his shoulder.

"Every universe in the multiverse must be lining up in just the right way. They are all synched with the deal that I just offered. As long as everything is synched, anyone and anything can effortlessly travel through different portions of reality. We are in quantum coherence."

"All of that science is beautiful, but what about that?" The Devil and Jack watched as the blue light melted a 39-point star onto the ground, summoning you into this new reality. "We are dead!"

"My sentiments exactly!" you screeched back at him. You were only a few moments away from tearing them limb from limb. You thought it would be fun to leave them with just an arm, so you could watch them try to scramble away.

What had once been *Bland* music etched into a CD quickly turned into a symphony of 1,001 electric guitars and a lone bass. This was the music of death. These jams would replace your old CD, and it would have a solo with a kazoo. The ball instilled its energy up your arm, and you readied it to be passed through your hand.

Choice S

YOU HAD BEEN casually hunting butterflies through the fields of dandelions and bunnies when a portal below the register mat you were standing on opened. A red demon with golden hair stepped causally from the portal first, and you watched her contemplate what village she was going to snuff out next. Then as you watched, she let out a fiery groan. She ripped open another portal and pulled a pale orc wielding a tiny battle ax from the new portal. You had no idea what was going on. It was likely some home spell gone wrong, given that the area you were in was off limits from demon spawn.

You watched them talk, letting your arrow hover between your eye and their forms. This wasn't the sort of thing that usually happened. In fact, if you hadn't taken a break from working at your shop, you could have avoided this. It wasn't the time to be taking chances with demons or orcs, especially with the nearby village being full of young blood that could easily power either one of them. Granted, you were not some kind of racist like normal cashiers your age. You weren't going to shoot two seemingly innocent Agents of Darkness without proper cause. What if they were both here just to have a lover's spat or to pick dandelions? Even evil people probably saw beauty in the world sometimes.

Though as you continued to watch them both, you saw a bright blue light melt through the dandelions. As it receded there was a bright blue demon, glowing brighter than the two-mooned sky, when the Goddess of the Moon was confused about how many moons there should be in the sky. The answer was always Two and a Half Moons.

The Blue Demon spoke to the pale orc, and it began to summon an energy that crackled the air in your lungs. If ol' Blue was able to project that energy through your newfound friends, then it would certainly destroy the fields. If the fields were destroyed, you had no idea how you were going to feed your family.

Distantly, you could hear the growling of 1001 bears with asthma and one lonely badger with a cough. It had replaced the sound you typically heard in the distance, a hissing snake with a lisp, a bow string being plucked, and the sizzling flesh of an animal over fire. You were going to have to put a stop to Blue. The other villains hadn't even been doing anything sinister.

You had two arrows that were given to you after your last quest. The Keeper of the Chest had called the arrows the most powerful weapon on your side of the multiverse. They were capable of cutting any living being. You had been saving one of the arrows specifically for the

Dark Overlord threatening your village, but the other was fare game. As long as you still thought you could kill the Dark Lord with a single shot, which you did. It wasn't like he had various pieces of his soul in different places, so that he could artificially extend his life, while slowly losing his humanity, because that would hardly be believable.

You held the arrow between two of your fingers and placed it into the bowstring. While pulling the bowstring back, you realized that if you missed this shot, it would be the end either way. You took a deep breath, and you felt the blue energy cracking the air in your lungs. Your fingers snapped away, and the arrow didn't move.

In reality, nothing moved at all. By accident, you had used the time stopping arrow. You had meant to never use it, but that was difficult enough, when you were cursed to keep it inside of your quiver. The rule was that time would stand still until you exhaled. You let your bow hang in mid-air, and you dived from the top of your perch.

It was difficult, but you were able to hold your breath in your lungs. You pushed the pale orc and the red demon out of the line of sight from the blue energy. Once everything seemed perfectly placed, you exhaled. The arrow, which had been storing up potential energy while time was paused, converted every ounce of it into kinetic energy. The kinetic energy latched onto the arrow like fire, and it exploded towards ole Blue.

The arrow struck Blue with a heavy smack and tore the flesh from its bones. A large orb fell onto the ground, and once it bounced back up, Blue reformed with deformed limbs.

"So, you thought that you could just kill me, huh?" Blue said.

"Yes." You pulled the unstoppable arrow, that you had originally meant to shoot at the blue demon, from the quiver and pulled it into the bowstring. You were actually able to shoot the arrow, but 'Ol Blue had consumed and absorbed the time energy from the arrow you had actually shot. The Blue Demon reversed time and used its tail to face you towards the pale orc.

The arrow snapped from your bow, because you were unable to stop the action and it smashed through the orc's hand that was wrapped around the handle of his battle axe. "Lumber be damned!" he screamed. Blood squirted from his hand, coating nearby dandelions, but he couldn't pull his hand away from the arrow.

"Still think you can stop me? I hope not, but I can see why you would want to try. You want to be the hero, but what you don't realize is that these two attacked me first. I'm just getting vengeance," 'Ole Blue said.

"Vengeance is never the right path."

"Blah blah blah. I think I am better than everyone because I look like Robin Hood. Can you guess who I am?"

"A blue demon trying to destroy everything in the universe?"

"I was doing an impression of you," the Blue Demon said, rolling its eyes.

"You aren't very good at them!"

"Perhaps, I'll work on that when there is nothing left in this universe!" The blue energy enters your lungs again, and it was enough to shred one of them.

"Should we help him?" the pale orc asked, but the red demon shook her head.

"We have no obligation to this universe or any universe," then she vanished through another portal. The pale orc made fleeting eye contact with you, but ultimately, he stepped towards the portal. Despite your good intentions, he was going to leave you to die. It made sense, given that he was a dirty orc hanging out with a red demon. As the pale orc passed through the portal, he hesitated, screamed, and chopped the portal in half with his ax.

"I am not leaving you here!"

"What are you going to do then?" The Blue Demon asked. It shot blue energy, like lightning, towards the brave orc, but he deflected it with his ax blade. The words from the Blue Demon's mouth slowly crawled back down its throat, when they realized what the pale orc was going to do.

The Lumberjack broke his ax over his knee, and he held his fists out. The arrow was still very much through the center of his palm. The sliver tip of it had fully torn through the backside of his hand.

"You can't be serious…."

"I can and am. If I land a punch, you have to take the final kill shot."

'Ole Blue flickered as demonic energy pulsed over its body. The demonic energy turned the demon's hair into a long flowing main of golden power. Then the demon's blue skin turned bright purple.

"Super Demon God mode. I'm more powerful than the Devil herself." 'Ole blue, now more of 'Ole purple, flew into the air, and two tiny serrated disks of plasma appeared. "If these touch, they'll will kill you."

"We'll see," the Lumberjack said.

'Ole purple launched one of the disks of plasma, and as it passed through both space and time, the air it touched became grey and lifeless. You knew that the demon wasn't boasting claims of untruth, but even so, the disks weren't aimed at the Lumberjack. Instead, the discs were moving towards you. You deflected the spinning plasma with your bow, but they sliced the bow in two complete halves. You had a repair spell, but as you grabbed your bow, it melted.

"I think you get the point," 'Ole purple said.

The demon teleported behind the Lumberjack, and struck him across the back with one of his discs. Blood splattered across the field, but you didn't have a weapon to help. The man tried to help you, but you were just going to stand idly by.

The Lumberjack smashed his hand across 'Ole purple's chest, and the tip of your arrow went directly into the demon's right lung. It let out a wicked scream that caught nearby flowers on fire.

"Kill it. Kill it now!" the Lumberjack said.

You were still armless, so you weren't sure how to kill a purple demon that you had just met for the first time. Then you realized that the blade of the ax was lying on the ground. You dived for it and slung it at the demon. It struck the demon in the chest, but the image you saw shifted and morphed, and you realized that what you had struck was actually the Lumberjack.

The once mythical creature fell forward onto his face. Lumberjacks were now the completely extinct. The flowers were soaked in blood, and the field became absent of bunnies. You weren't going to be feeding your family on this night.

"Made a mistake did ya?" The demon pulsed with fantastical energy that it morphed into a magical spinning blade of death. If it killed you, sure you would die, but it would be a magical death. It would be like dying by being impaled by a unicorn. Sure, it sucked that you were clearly going to die by bleeding to death, but you had also just discovered the unicorn. Bleeding to death wasn't nearly as bad as discovering unicorns were real.

"Say goodnight everybody." The serrated disk of fiery red plasma was launched at a speed you could hardly understand. Watching it gave it less momentum, and it ended up smashing into the ground in front of you, causing the Earth to open up and swallow you.

"You missed!" you screamed up to the purple demon

The demon looked down at you, but you continued to fall. "I didn't miss, you are on your way to Hell. Have fun."

Your soundtrack began to twist and pull away from you. It merged with the sound of an out of tune banjo, and it became literal torture as you continued to fall further and further towards the lava-ridden Hellscape.

Time passed beyond the chasm of cataclysm. You could see your world becoming older and worn. The sunflowers soaked in blood, dropped onto the ground that you could no longer see. Eventually, the cold blue sky was glazed over with orange embers of eternal fire. While in your personal Hellscape, you had to run a machine within a trade post that attempted to register the amount of gold shillings you were given. *Ding.* Hand them more money. You were also forced by some ethereal force that you never say, but always heard to ask your patrons if they wanted to save an amount of shillings by signing up for a rectangular piece of metal. You had no idea how the madness would end. At the very least, it appeared you were unable to age, despite being scarred from your first moments in the Hellscape.

Once you were at your thirteenth job, where you mined screaming rubies from rocks that looked like the heads of people, you noticed something glimmering beyond the rock. Just beyond the rock, you could see the neck of a guitar, waiting for you. You felt your options shift within in the air, cracking and settling. You could go for the guitar which was an option. But, it felt sort of like you were going to be turned into a stone filled with screaming rubies if you tried. You could also continue to slowly deteriorate.

They were equally viable options. Still, you felt that

there had to be another option. When you had infinite time and nothing left to lose, you would have assumed there were more than exactly two options. As always, you were absolutely correct. There were in fact, approximately two options. An approximation allows for the possibility of a third option, and a third option was what you really needed.

Instead, you planned. You planned on grabbing the guitar and playing the *Song of Teleportation*. That was as soon as you remembered how it went. It had been taught to you by a monk dressed in a suit made of candy, and even though it hadn't worked for you, you had paid an outrageous amount of money for the music sheets. He promised you that, "It definitely works," and you had no reason to not believe him. After all, he had seven teeth, and seven was a lucky number.

You grabbed the neck of the guitar, trying to choke the song out of it. You played the noted that you remembered as fast as possible, before the demon that was watching over you noticed. Then you sang the teleportation song.

"The teleportation song." The demon that was nearby ran towards you, the fiery red whip appearing at his side coated in fire. You felt the lightning pulse through your body, and you mashed upwards through the crack in Mother Earth's face. You landed on the lip of the chasm back in the field.

Instead of having sunflowers, the field was actually coated in grey snow that was falling from the sky. Except when you attempted to catch a snowflake on your tongue, you found that it was ash. Ash was falling from the sullen sky and coating the ground as eternal winter. You stumbled through the ash covered field, creating footsteps in the ash.

You tripped over the skeleton of the Lumberjack. The ax was no longer inside of his chest, but it looked like it had recently been taken from it. You were now without a weapon and without knowledge. It would have been easy to out think your opponent, given you knew anything, but now you couldn't even defend your inability to know something.

As you stumbled through the ash and moved above the ridge, you saw your town. It was engulfed in a spectacular fire. Though it was fun to look at, and generally beautiful, fire was not the natural state of your town. Really, the natural state of your town was partially sunny and not on fire.

The fire looked as though it had already consumed everything you knew. Your album gained an additional track, a sad piano. It played a melody that would have made anyone cry, but you weren't just anyone. Your town, and perhaps even your family, had burned to the ground. There was nothing here for you now.

The sad piano continued with each footstep. You continued walking, sad piano in the background. You walked passed the *Forest of Staleen*. You walked passed the *Woods of No More Ideas*. And finally, you walked passed the *Swamp of Convenience*.

It was at the Swamp that you saw 'Ole Purple sinking into the steamy waters. Legend foretold that the swamp was such a place where any traveler may find the thing most convenient for themselves. There were tales of people who had come to the swamp with ailments and leave completely healthy. You had even heard similar stories about people who wandered into the swamp by accident, seeking to drink from it, only to be greeted by a beautiful waterfall. Whether the stories were true or not was always the topic of discussion amongst drunk historians.

You were partially afraid about what might happen if you approached the swamp. There was no telling what you needed the most. Did you need the cure to a Hellscape virus? Did you need a new bow? Did you need a manager's key? Who knew?

The water in the swamp splashed and thrashed, and 'Ole Purple moved back out of the water. The demon was holding the orball again. Except this time, it looked to be 26 small orballs morphed into one single product.

"Finally," 'Ole Purple screeched.

You slipped behind a tree as the demon passed through a portal. Across the front of the tree, letters began to appear in the bark. *Open the Ark of the Convenient.* An arrow appeared across the front of every tree in your direct vicinity, pointing towards a glowing chest across the swamp. You moved effortlessly towards the other side, and you placed your hand against the cold brass handle. 'Ole Purple jumped from a portal on the other side of the chest.

"Don't do it. If you open that chest, I will kill you. It is plain and simple." You began to open the chest, but

'Ole Purple glared at you, the intensity itself was enough to hold you in place. "You better hope that whatever is in that chest will kill me once you use it." What were the odds though, you wondered?

"Did you know your world has a replay button that just grows on trees? A treeplay button?" you asked.

Your moment ran short, and then the ark was completely cracked open. Inside of it, there was a dark blue light filled with an orange cream filling.

The ark was filled to the brim with nothing, which was convenient, but not for you specifically. You weren't sure who it was convenient for, but you realized in that moment, that anything was convenient for someone else. If the gun had no bullets, it was convenient for the person being shot at. If the gun has bullets, it was convenient for the person shooting. If the gun was filled with bullets that summoned the Devil, then it was convenient for the Devil. If the bullets were tiny suicidal flea people…

You weren't sure who would benefit from you not having an amazing weapon that could stop someone who seemed like the literal Devil. If you could stop her before more time passed, you wouldn't have to suffer through more problems. What were you going to do about 'Ole Purple though? That thing was standing behind the ark looking at it like it was the start of a magic act. It clearly was not.

You pulled the nothing out of the air and aimed it at 'ole purple. The demon was taken aback at first, probably because you were acting aggressive. 'Ole Purple backed away from you, not really willing to fight nothing. The demon was opposed to the idea that you could be holding any amount of invisible objects. Granted you were not holding anything, but 'Ole Blue didn't know that quite yet.

"I will shoot! Do not underestimate me!" you screamed as you pointed your arms even straighter towards the demon. This was your last stand. You had no idea what you were going to do after the demon figured out what you were doing, but that wasn't important in that moment.

"I would never underestimate myself," 'Ole Purple said. The demon twisted its hand around, so that you could see your fingertips on the underside of the demon's hands.

"This isn't possible," you said.

"Quite a bit of things aren't possible. Flight. Time travel. Lying. These were all concepts of the impossible. And yet," 'Ole Purple began to rise into the air, and then another version of the demon rose to its side. "Everything will be okay," the demon said to its other self. As the sentence finished, the new version of the demon stabbed the old, and that version fell. It was dead at your feet in an instance.

"How?'

"The question is why not? I know you have nothing. I know there's nothing you can do to stop me. This ark is nothing." 'Ole Purple gained an aura that melted the individual carbon atoms in the air, making it rain shards of red light. "I have to kill you now. Sorry about that." 'Ole Purple went to strike you, but the ark became conveniently conscious and grabbed the demon by its wrists.

"What is this madness?" you both said.

The ark shifted and morphed into a boombox, and it began to play a loud solo trumpet. It only took you a moment to realize that it was a charge sound. The ark pulsed a single wormhole of light, and the archangel Michael, and an angel, who could have been named, Rhonda, smashed through the portal. They grabbed 'Ole Purple as they continued through the portal. Each of them took a portion of 'Ole Purple's shoulder, and slammed it into the ground.

"That's how Heaven does it," the Rhonda angel said. 'Ole Purple let out a magical laugh that boomed loud enough to destroy the ground. It opened enough to pull the demon through to the next dimension.

Then you realized that your chest was punctured by one of the orballs. Blood was pulsing down your shirt and pooling on the ground. Rhonda ran over to you, and she caught you just as you fell to the ground. She held you over her outstretched wing and smiled down at you. "It's okay. This wasn't the time. There will be another time."

She lifted her hand up to your face, and she had a nail that was long and pointed. It was yellowed with age, and as she touched it to your face it was rough and sharp. She dragged it across your face, and you could feel another track being etched into your existence and your album.

It sounded like funeral music. Slow drums, bagpipes, and a screeching flute. "We will help you. We are always here for you." The world flashed black and your options were blacked out.

Choice T

THE DEVIL WAS offering you a deal for your soundtrack, but you were too concentrated on your work. You waved her away. It was possible that you would wave someone away even if they weren't the literal Devil. You had work. You had a quota. Every thirty-seven seconds a barcode had to be scanned or you lost approximately half a millimeter of your height.

Even when you weren't shrinking, your job had a way of making you feel small. It felt like when you had started working there you were eight feet tall, and you had a soul. Now, it felt like two inches of one had been bled out of you and the other was just diced.

Work. Work. Work. Work. Work. It was surprising that wasn't one of your songs on your album. The Devil approached you again, but you were unsure if it was the same day.

"How can I help you?" you said.

"*I want your soul,*" the thing slurred at you.

It was the kind of voice that you had never heard.

You looked up, and you saw a purple colored creature. It smiled at you with a wicked lack of gums. This was something in your handbook that they had warned you about.

A purple colored Demon may one day finally come to see you. It has been coming for the last 100 years to this location. Luckily, we have been taking precautions on the off chance that it will come back again. The scanner on your register has two modes. Scan, which does the obvious scanning of barcodes. It is hardly harmful to people, either mildly irritating them or giving them small amounts of poisonous radiation. Whichever, it will not kill them in the moment and no one will be able to blame you, and that's the Shop Awesome Guarantee.

The other mode, activated by double clicking the trigger is a shotgun that shoots laser rounds that instantly disintegrate any living creature that it touches. Obviously, this mode is the one you will use to fight the Purple Demon, or the Devil, if you are to see her.

At the same time, if you accidentally kill someone, do not fret. You are allowed thirteen murders per year, before the police will be called on you. That's the Shop Awesome Guarantee.

Quickly, you double tapped the trigger on the scanner, and it transformed into a huge plastic shotgun. It seemed entirely too heavy for what it was made of, but it was going to have to do. You cocked it and locked your dead eye stare onto the Purple Demon.

"You think that is going to kill me? That weak toy?"

You nodded. "It isn't a toy. It is a gun." You flicked

your finger across the trigger, and a laser blasted into the sky. A red laser smashed through the ceiling and continued flashing into the sky until it was a red dot above you.

The Purple Demon lifted the orball up, and you thought you could see it pulsing like a heart. It flickered, reflecting the purple Demon's teeth.

"If you aren't careful, you will get everyone killed."

The employee manual stated directly across the front that the company would cover a lawsuit in Demon court, but at the cost of your health insurance. At the same rate, if you were dead, health insurance wouldn't be particularly helpful. It was sort of a catch 22. The orball expanded a bit more, and you could already feel your mortal soul being pulled towards its center.

You weighed your options, considering them slowly. On one hand, you had your watch, provided by the company. It was there to remind you both the weight of your job and to be on time. On the other hand, you had your fingers wrapped around a laser pistol. One of the choices was the correct choice. You took the shot, and the laser round smashed through the orball.

"That is an unfavorable choice." The orball exploded into shrapnel that could tear the very fabric of reality. A small shard smashed through your chest, delivering a fateful fatal blow. It was like time had forced the winds of change through the window of opportunity and directly through your specific flame. You were no more.

Choice U

"CASHIERING! CASHIERING! CASHIERING! There's nothing cooler than being a cashier! I could be a firefighter or I could be a fighter fire. Nothing would compare to being a cashier! Cashier with no fear! I could smash a vase and feel no pain! No need to explain, I'm just a cashier on a roll." As you continued singing, a deep pang rocketed through your heart. It felt like a version of yourself in the great cosmos had been destroyed. Granted, it didn't matter, because you didn't believe in alternate universes.

You pulled a small calculation device from your pocket. Upon its front was a single letter U. You didn't need to believe in alternate universes, because you knew that they were real. There were approximately 27 universes overall. Each of them was directly beside the next one. You had only felt the pang in your heart one other time, and it had been because the version of you had died tragically. Luckily, he didn't die, because that would have hurt much worse. As far as you could tell, you were one of the few versions of you linked to the others.

"I don't have time for this." You set down your scanner. You pulled off your badge and set it onto the counter. "Excuse me. This is my one ticket out of here."

Without looking back, you ran towards your car. If your watch was wound correctly, it looked as though a demon was going to be showing up in 45 seconds. It felt like one of your previous versions was dying in one of the realities to the left of yours. You were sure that the realties to the right would be equipped to handle it. You popped your trunk, and inside was the sharpened ax guitar. It had been handed down from one lumberjack to the next, along with the *Bland* soundtrack.

The reason that it was so bland was so that you didn't attract unwanted attention from your real soundtrack. You lifted the strap over your head, and you started shredding metal. You actually shredded metal so well, that it shredded the metal of your car, revealing a suit of power armor on the interior. With a simple click of the unlock button, the armor leaped forward and wrapped itself around you. You looked like a space samurai.

The gateway opened directly behind you, and the demon stepped out. You had yet to encounter this particular demon, but as it turned about, you could see that it was just a purple version of your own face. You looked devilishly good looking.

"Fancy meeting you here," 'Ol Purple said.

"What do you want?" you asked the demon.

"Do I need to want something? Can I not come visit myself in the *oh so distant possibility?*"

"I'd prefer you stayed in whatever Hell Hole you crawled out of."

"That is very self-destructive of you."

"Go to Hell."

"Only if you come with me," he said back to you.

You were left staring at each other. Somehow, you both knew what was happening, but unfortunately neither of you were quite confident of what to do next.

The Purple Demon produced a small orb/ball. You weren't quite sure which one it was. Mostly, because it was clearly both.

"I'll give you to the count of ten. One, two, three—"

"Let me help you. Ten," you screamed. Completely caught off guard, 'Ol Purple didn't quite know what to do next, but times had changed and you had some idea what to do. You struck the guitar as hard as you could, and the sound waves created daggers in the air. They soared through the air, but the demon could not be struck. Somehow it was immune to your ax. It didn't take you long to realize that it was because you could not injure yourself with your own weapon.

"I'm going to take your weapon," 'Ol Purple said with a huge smile. In that moment, you knew you were screwed, but at the same time, you had been solemnly sworn to protect the multiverse. In the distance, you heard the different universe reeving to demolish yours. You had very, very little time to act. It wouldn't be long before they sent an inter-dimensional missile to destroy your whole universe.

Beyond just time, you just had very, very few options. If you were going to guess how many options you actually had, you would have expected none. Interestingly, the word none had one in it. You were going to go for that option. You opted for the N one.

This was going to be your last action, so you really had to make it count. With just your pinky tip, you snapped a string from your guitar. The sudden action caused the whole of reality to freeze. You had broken the one ax. Since that ax was said to be unbreakable, you had frozen the Universe in a never ending cycle of self-doubt. It was probably how the Titanic felt when it was sinking. You, like the captain of the Titanic, were going to go down with your ship. And you, like the captain of the Titanic, were frozen in place. Unlike the captain of the Titanic, you were not part of a disaster at sea, but you were part of the sinking of your reality. Though time was frozen, you still had plenty of time to think about what was going to happen. You could easily stay frozen, staring at the purple version of yourself, but eternity was forever. At the same time, time was also a human construct. There was no telling if there was a beginning, middle, or end.

This thought was the one that pushed you to actualization. You became stronger than the concept of the universe and its existence in time. Just like gravity, you bent time to your will. Ol' Purple began to age so rapidly that they gained the d in old. Hair grew from every pore of the demon's body, in spurts of onion yellow. Smelling strangely of red onions. Then with one final push, you used your time manipulation to destroy Old Purple. Then the demon collapsed into a pile of coarse, maroon dust.

"Got you." Unfortunately, as much as you wanted to enjoy the new demon free world, you were too strong for the universe. You were too strong for time. Instead, you joined the other superior gods. Warren, Chuck, Jones, and Xanose. The four greats beyond the possibility of possible. Never were you to go back to earth. Nor did you care to care about the humans. They were worse off than when they were Norse of course.

Once in a great while, you heard the distant song of the cashier. You needed no music, because music directly needed time to matter. By sacrificing everyone in the universe you had trapped the in thing that could have destroyed everything at the core of the universe. The purple demonic version of yourself was never going to make it to the 26th universe and that meant you were a hero.

Though you would never know it, people in the other stable universes praised your bravery in the face of evil. Statues were designed in your image. In some universes, you had a festival that lasted an entire week.

You were trapped with only you as company. Perhaps that is irony.

Choice V

THE WORLD WAS always slightly more complicated than it let on. People seemed to enjoy depressing music, because it made them happy. Some disliked happy moments, because it made them think of sad music.

You liked to think that you were different. Maybe thinking that you were different was all that made you different. It was possible that here were only 20 or so variations of everything. You were sure that Doritos and Oreos were getting dangerously close to the edge. Still, you liked music, sad and happy. You aspired to become the world's greatest kazooist. The choice of kazoo rotated around the idea that no one sought to be the master of the kazoo, so you would have to try very little to be the best.

In fact, a couple years after you quit your job as a cashier at Soul Sucking International, you were the top kazooist in the nation. You played with the Great's on a nightly basis.

Monday, you had a gig with AC/DC where you played a solo for *Hells Bells* on the kazoo. Tuesday, you were with Beyoncé playing through her latest album. The days went on and on like this. It felt like the success would never end, and you knew that it wouldn't.

You had a dirty a secret, one that you wanted no one to be aware of forever. You were ashamed. You were a lesser musician.

While you worked at Soul Sucking International, you had taken a deal with the Devil. In exchange for your soul, you would become the best kazooist. The stipulation was that you could never touch another instrument or you would lose your life instantaneously. Though it was a harsh catch, it seemed easily avoided. You couldn't shake the idea that maybe the Devil was up to something. Then again, she was the Devil, it was her shtick to be up to something.

Then things got worse. Worse for everyone. The Devil had been planning a hostile take-over for quite some time. People stopped showing up to concerts, and over time, they retreated underground. It didn't take long for demons to climb from the bowels of the Earth, killing anything they saw. They seemed to have good vision, so they did an excessive amount of killing.

Eventually, even you would have to sleep under a rock, praying at night that Death wouldn't find you. One day, as you laid under the softest rock you could find, you heard some rustling in the bushes beyond. That wasn't good news. Try as you might, you couldn't cease to exist within a completely two-dimensional space.

The rock began to move and you said your last prayer. Except it wasn't a demon, it was a winged man. He was standing there, holding an ax. If you hadn't seen the wings first, you might have thought him to be a lumberjack given his beard and flannel.

"I take it you're going to hide here until you die," he said. His eyes narrowed on you until you felt small enough to fit under the rock again. Luckily, that was in your imagination. The angel didn't have legitimate shrinking powers. He probably didn't have illegitimate ones either.

"I was planning on staying until I was killed, not until I die. They are going to find me, just like you did." You clutched your rock even closer to your body.

"How about instead, you take this ax and fight?" the JackAngel said.

"Because fighting is for brave people?"

"Don't kid yourself, kid. You are clearly brave." He held the handle out to you and you were tempted to grab it, but something stopped you.

"No. I'd rather throw a rock at them or something. Can you find your own rock?"

"Can you… not suck so much?" The Angel said to you, bringing the handle even closer to your face.

"You know what? Fine!" You grabbed the handle, but as soon as your hands gripped the solid mahogany, your heart suddenly stopped. Beyond your body, the Devil appeared, a smile playing across her lips.

"Instrument of Destruction," she said as she ran her

finger across the broadside of the blade. As she pulled her finger away, it was smoking. She blew the smoke away and her smile returned.

"What did you do, Demon?" The Bearded Angel went to swing his ax, but he was unable to move.

"To you or the chosen one?"

"Both."

"You are paralyzed. And as for the chosen one, I told him that if he touched another instrument, he would die instantly. Unfortunately, I didn't tell him which instrument. Seems as though he thought it was all of them, but it was just that one. Not even a musical instrument."

"You are not gonna get away with this. The ax will find its way." The Devil rolled her eyes.

"Did you go to the exposition school of expositional phrases? Gonna tell me your plan now?"

"I thought you might tell me yours if I stalled."

"You thought wrong," she said. With one final look, she vanished amongst the trees, leaving the angel by himself, waiting for something.

"Only three more," the Devil whispered from the distance.

"You won't get away with this!" the Lumberjack Angel screamed.

"Generic hero says what?"

"You will never get away with this!" the Lumberjack Angel said again.

"That's what they all say."

Choice W

ADEAL WITH THE Devil had been offered to you, and you could take it. Really, it wasn't much different than everything else you sold your soul for. Certain social media was really only free because you were selling everything but your soul. Your data. Your habits. Your favorite movie. Everything. Those were all for sale somewhere. Why wouldn't the essence of your being be for sale too? The companies didn't even have to trick you into buying into false pretense either. Every time a new software update came out, you instinctively agreed, because you wanted music. You wanted to be able to say the word *selfie,* and said selfie be taken, and you wanted access to things that never cost you money.

In return, companies want to know what you listen to, and how often you take pictures.

"You can have it," you said, sliding the contract back.

"What do you mean?" The Devil asked. Her demeanor had changed from manipulative to confused.

"I mean take it. It's yours, I don't really have a use for it, right?"

The Devil was taken aback. Never in her thousands of years did someone offer their soul instead of taking a deal. Her fingernails extended into long talons that moved towards your chest. The talons wrapped around your soul and pulled back. For a moment, you could see the wiggling blue mass moving from your flesh. She continued pulling, but your soul snapped back into your body.

"What's wrong?" You asked.

"I can't take it. Why can't I take it?" She pulled again, but your soul was firmly latched to your body. *Pop!* A bright white window appeared in front of you with black lettering across the front. **Terms and Services.**

"What is this?" you asked. The Devil shrugged, looking at the window with you.

"I've never seen this before," she said.

You agree to lose your soul. In return, you will gain access to Hell. In Hell, you will find everything fits your ultimate displeasure. You gain the inability to be tortured by traditional means by agreeing to this contract.

Have you read the terms and services?

Next to that question, there was a checkbox with the word yes inside of it. You reached out, conscious of all the eyes on you. Everyone was impatiently tapping their feet, waiting to check out a salt lamp. Meanwhile, you were having a crisis to the point that you were selling your soul to the Devil.

You checked the box and the window dissipated into a mass of cool, blue smoke. The cash register clicked open and a stairwell appeared in the till. From your position, you couldn't see the bottom, but you could see orange light near the end. You lifted your leg up into the register and descended into the depths of Hell.

Really, it wasn't that bad. The stairwell was perhaps a few degrees over room temperature. On your trip down, you passed by a couple of layers of people suffering. There were the people screaming while getting ice cream. There was another layer dedicated to people having a pillow fight in agonizing, bloody pain. You could only imagine that the pillows were filled with rusty nails. There was even a layer for cooking class, where souls were condemned to bake cupcakes.

At the bottom of the stairs, the Devil was waiting for you in front of a large oak door. She was tapping her watch and pacing.

"What took you so long?" she asked.

"I had to walk through Hell to get here."

"What? That place you just came from? That's just Hell for the masochists. They can't be tortured, because that wouldn't work. We created a surface level to Hell that acts a bit like Heaven to torture the self-harming weirdos."

Looking back, you could hear a faint voice screaming, "Someone just hit me, please!" It made sense, but you had never thought about what happened to masochists when they went to Hell.

"What if they go to Heaven?" you asked. The Devil let out a bellowing laugh that dropped pebbles from the ceiling.

"If. If. If." She threw open the door to reveal a sudden drop into a deep red pit of fire and brimstone. It wafted angrily with the sound of death and pain. "Isn't it beautiful?" she asked.

"No?"

"You don't think? You'll learn. Or maybe you won't, it will be fun to find out." The Devil snapped her fingers and a golden scepter appeared in her hand. She passed it off to you, and for moment, you felt a flicker of something in your chest. For once, you felt.

"What's this?"

"The one willing to give their soul away is worthy of ruling a portion of Hell. That was in the terms and services that I signed. I never read it before." The Devil said. Her frown flicked upwards into a hesitant smile. She pressed her hand into your back, "You'll do well."

Just like that, she pushed you into the pit of Hell, and you fell to your demise. Except death would have been a typical torture, also against the rules. Instead, you landed neck first into the ground, and you were instantly paralyzed.

Lying on your back for eternity, you did have people to govern like the Devil promised, but not to the extent you thought. You ruled over a small family of ants.

You managed their microscopic lives. You tried to keep them organized, fed, and loved. Over time, they grew to hate you, thinking you to be a malevolent King, and they left you. Your time alone wasn't painful in itself, but it was exhausting. The worst part was that you couldn't even go somewhere else to find more ants to rule over. This is what your afterlife would be like forever.

Choice X

YOUR CASHIER JOB was one of those things that you had to endure. It bought you food and food gave you energy or something and that allowed you to do your job. Your job allowed you to buy food, which allowed you to have energy to work at your job to buy food. It wasn't as cyclomatic as you thought. It was in fact necessary for life to continue. Sort of like the circle of life or the life cycle. It was exactly as cyclomatic as you thought.

Regardless, one time, when you were at your job at Corporate Job Inc. using your half scanner/death-ray, you saw the Devil waiting in your line. It was strange that she thought she could get you. She had tried to borrow/steal your soul a couple dozen or so times. Everyone was wise to the Devil's tricks. It was probably because of that whole forcing a guy named Bobby to eat an apple of knowledge and pissing off his girlfriend.

"What do you want?" you asked the Devil.

"Your death," she mumbled.

"What?"

"Your death!" She yanked an ax from her purse and swung it around towards you. You leaned back casually and it sliced a few strands of hair from your head. They fell to the counter and burst in flames.

"Class 5 cursed object? That is against the rules, and you know it."

"I'm the Devil, not the IRS." She swung the ax again, but you used your scanner to blind her. "I'm going to kill you!" Another swing, but she was unable to hit you.

You jumped onto the counter and unscrewed your arm from your body. You slapped the Devil as hard as you could with it and she nicked it with her ax, then you placed it on her head. It exploded with such force she was launched backwards into a Pepsi machine.

"You aren't capable of defeating me!" she screamed. She opened a Pepsi and took a nice refreshing drink and looked to the camera. "If you want to have a nice shield against devilish forces, drink Pepsi, because it doesn't leave a weird taste in your mouth like Coke."

"This isn't an advertisement."

"Why not?" She stood, wiping the Pepsi from the corners of her mouth. You reached under the counter and grabbed your secondary arm. Your hands wrapped around the intercom, and you could feel the electricity move through it.

"Death is in sector B. Defensive positions, everyone."

"You think they can stop me? With what army?"

"That is a classic line. Too bad it won't help anything."

You took the energy from the intercoms, feeling the energy feed into your arms and legs. It slashed through your body and turned your hair a bright white.

"What are you saying?" the Devil asked you, but you were busy draining electricity from the walls.

"I'm saying that I'm going to kill you." You shot a bolt of lightning from your fingertips, and it passed through the devil's chest. It sliced the fleshy look off her body and revealed the really real red flesh of the Devil. She was just the biblical Devil in the form of a woman.

"I'm not letting this slide." She pounced forward, but as she jumped into the air the first part of a dance song started to play on your track. These precious few notes were enough of a dancy jive to get your body moving slightly to the left. She soared over you and crashed into the cash register. Two quarters fled the machine, and you caught them with your off hand, or your on hand, because you used that one too.

The Devil stood back up, her horns glimmering with fresh blood. As she spoke, her voice had deepened. "You're going to regret that very soon." With a thought, she discarded the ax. It rested blade down, handle up on the floor.

You, on the other hand, flung one of the quarters with such force that it slammed into the Devil's temple. It hit her and flicked off into the distance.

"Ouch! What the hell did you just throw at me?"

"A quarter. A twenty-five-cent piece as it were."

"Why?"

"It's the weapon in my hand."

"Could've punched me." A little bit of blood trailed down the Devil's face.

"That would've been too easy." You smiled.

"Kind of a douchey thing to do."

"What do you care? Aren't you the Devil? Be an adult." You flicked the other quarter, but the Devil dropped to the floor before it could hit her.

"Good try." Even though you missed, your track changed. It switched to an upbeat brass and huge stringed orchestra.

"I didn't miss."

The Devil twisted around to look. The quarter struck a shelf holding several vases. It cracked a single glass shelf, but it didn't stay cracked for long. The sheer weight from all the vases caused the shelf to snap clean in half. Then the shelf fell atop The Devil, pinning her for a moment. Vases exploded for effect.

Your vision locked into the ax that you couldn't touch, then it locked onto the door. It would have been relatively easy to run. You didn't owe it to anyone to fight the Devil. In fact, you hardly cared about this dimension. This lousy dimension didn't have ice cream, which meant you'd have to invent it, but if you invented it, you were sure that you would rip the very nature of existence. However, that was a very small price to pay for some good ice cream.

Run. You thought to yourself. But what would you do? How would you do it? You'd run away with a cashier's salary. What then? Were you going to go to the far off exotic land of your next door neighbor's house? Face it, you aren't that great of a person.

You eyeballed the door, despite your INNER VOICE telling you not to. You knew it was a stupid idea to run. Running would only end in sadness. What you needed to do was pick up the ax and charge the Devil, even if that meant certain death. SOMEHOW, YOU WERE ABLE YOU IGNORE YOUR INNER VOICE ENTIRELY, AND YOU SAUNTERED TOWARDS THE DOOR.

Where the hell did you think you were going? Everything you were doing was against the plot! Everything you were doing was against the will of the creator. If you didn't come back right now, then there were going to be terrible consequences. And even though you CLEARLY knew that, you didn't stop walking towards the door. You abandoned your mission and the opportunity to make a difference in the multiverse. Sort of a multi-purpose.

You continued walking towards a nightmare you created for yourself. You wandered into the unknown, unsure of the future. As you passed through the door into the grand Oasis beyond, it was then that you were struck by lightning and killed instantly. You were reduced to nothing, and that same nothing floated off into the distance.

Choice Y

THE MUSIC. IT sounded so real as if it were playing from a microscopic CD player in your head. Then you heard the jingle of change. Or as the cashiers of the land called it, the 50/50 split. This was the kind of moment that defined a person. It was the kind of moment where things could go heads up or belly down.

Someone that you had yet to meet walked to your counter with their head down. They muttered words that sounded like Spanish, but could have easily been Latin or Portuguese. It didn't help that you knew none of those languages. The new person at your counter smiled from under her cloak.

She fumbled in her purse and pushed a slip of paper in your direction. It wasn't money. It wasn't a check. It was a contract. The solemn woman wanted to buy your soundtrack. How did she know that you were part of a band? Why didn't the contract have any indication of how much you were being paid?

"For how much? The Lumberjacks don't play for free." You stopped. "Sometimes we play for free drinks."

"Anything you want," she said. Cryptic, but good.

"Two mill."

"Whatever you want."

"Four mill"

"Whatever you want."

"Five mill and free drinks."

"If this is what you want, then sign on the dotted line." She pressed a pen across the table and you signed it without reading it. Somehow, you didn't know that contracts to create music weren't as loose as iTunes terms and agreements contracts. In fact, you saw your mistake as the pen burned the paper instead of writing on it. You had just made a deal with the Devil.

Her wicked mouth opened, revealing rows and rows of teeth. A gust of wind pulled you towards her gullet, and your soul separated from your physically body like a carbon copy.

You looked back at the contract and back to the Devil. You needed to think of something fast, otherwise you were as good as dead.

"Before you take my *soundtrack*, don't you have to provide me with my five mill and my free drinks?" Loophole. Loophole. You needed one, but it would be too suspicious if you tried to use your lawyer summoning powers.

"Very well." She snapped her fingers and five towers of hundred-dollar bills appeared along with a margarita.

"Mind if I count this to make sure it is all here?"

"I'm a mythical being. This isn't wrong."

"If you're so mythical, then you can waste all the time in the world."

From there, you started counting all five million dollars. "4,999,990."

"That isn't possible. There's only hundreds in theses stacks," the devil said as she grew redder.

"Who are the courts going to side with? The definition of all evil or a cashier trained to count money?" She took another breath and manifested a ten-dollar bill to add to the stack.

"Better."

You hadn't seen that coming. She solved your problem, even though it didn't really make sense. You couldn't beat someone who was capable of such customer service. Her powers were much too strong for you to handle. She opened her mouth again, and your soul began pulling from your body again.

"Wait!"

"What is it this time?" she said, shutting her mouth and clicking her teeth back into place.

"I was supposed to get free drinks. But a margarita is one drink." She manifested another margarita, which you promptly drank.

"Better?"

"Not exactly. Two margaritas are actually the same free drink."

"What would you like instead?" Her patience was immeasurable. How were you ever going to defeat someone who could so easily trick you. *Think. Think. Think.*

"An ax grinder."

"I've never heard of it."

"That's because it's an... exclusive band drink."

"What's in it?"

"It's a whole banana mixed with vodka and yogurt. It is served inside the Holy Grail and stirred with a silver-plated dagger, left in as a garnish."

"I know this is a trap."

"So? If you know, you can stop it from happening. Seems simple enough, right?" She snapped her fingers and your drink appeared. Everything was frozen in place, maybe not literally, but you felt everything crispening at once like the cosmic butterfly net dropped you inside of the cosmic skillet. It all felt bizarre.

You grabbed the dagger, knowing full well that you couldn't move fast enough to strike the Devil. Your speed only allowed you to stir it slowly as you looked up at her. This was originally meant to be your last meal. A last meal that was an alcoholic beverage. The perfect last meal really. You get something into your stomach and you also get buzzed. Perfect.

You gripped the silver dagger, thinking very carefully about how you would approach the Princess of Darkness. It didn't really matter, because no matter what you did, you were going to die. Painfully. You, a cashier, versus the entity bent on putting everyone in her Hellscape. It wasn't going to end well.

"When do you think you will strike?" she asked you. You nodded, feeling the creaking of your neck.

"I'm thinking about it." There was a lot of money in front of you. It could help you escape. But how far away could you really go? Was the moon too far away?

Then in a flash of red light, you moved forward, blade outstretched. The plan? Strike the Devil in the chest and hope she exploded like a vampire. Even as everything blurred, you saw that she was poised to strike you back. This was it. You could see future dream memories of your head rolling around like a bizarre bowling ball.

She struck first, as expected, catching you across the temple. Yet, you didn't feel it. It didn't hurt, at least not you. The Devil's arm exploded off her body. Blood splattered across the walls, and you smashed the blade through her chest. The shock you experienced was paralyzing.

The Devil locked eyes with you, and you saw the glimmer of hellfire fade away from her sight. She slid off the blade and smacked the tile. You did it. Finally, you did it.

Game Over.

Everything faded into the green fog you hadn't seen. It slipped away and you noticed your head was heavy. It slumped forward under its own weight, and the green fog lifted as a helmet fell from your body.

It rolled into the new dank darkness of your life. Your eyes attempted a focus, but they shifted in and out, never fully getting what was there. Your attempts to move were hindered by chains. Hell, your attempts to speak were even hindered.

All that escaped your mouth when you spoke was a slight cloud of dust. You had no idea where you were, or what you were doing.

"Only took 25 different times." The lights flashed on, and the Devil was standing in front of you. She wasn't missing an arm, and she certainly was not dead like the last time you saw her.

"Because of you, I knew how to kill all of you. You were nothing to me. Glad you helped me though." It was then that you finally saw your state. Neither your arms nor your legs were attached to your body. You were instead suspended from the ceiling, hanging like a piñata. The helmet had rolled to the Devil, and she placed her foot atop it.

"So, I no longer have any use for you." She crushed the helmet, causing a slight tinge of pain in your head.

"If I said I was sorry, I'd be lying." Her pitchfork appeared in her hand, and she threw it at you. There was a brief moment where you wondered where everything went wrong, then the pitchfork seared itself through you. It melted through to the other side like a hot knife through a thin sheet of ice.

"Have a good life," she said with a wave.

Choice Z

A SMIDGE OF OXYGEN leaked into your lungs, and you came back to life. The cash register, which you expected, was not present. The soundtrack, which you expected to hear, was not present. Instead, you were lying down inside of a cracked glass tube. Your extremities felt numb, but other than that, you were unharmed.

Around you, caked in equal parts dust and darkness, were crates of limes. You peeled your bare back from the glass and slithered your way onto the cold cement. You didn't remember this reality or this universe. It wasn't one of the original 25 that you remembered.

In the far distance, you could vaguely hear an ominous organ. Your soundtrack must have been unfreezing somewhere separate. As soon as it caught back up to you, you'd have a better idea how much trouble you were in.

"Hello?" you screeched into the darkness, trying to stand on your rubbery legs.

"Hello," someone called back. The legs you had once trusted, now felt boneless, folding in on themselves.

"Who's out there?" Luckily, it didn't sound like the Devil had already found you. That would have been terrible. Instead, a lumberjack made its way to you. He had a nice burly beard, and a glimmering ax slung over his shoulder.

"The last lumberjack! Ever since the war, there can only be two. You were created to be the other one. We grew you in this tube, unsure of who you would become." It was then that you realized the room was triangular, almost like someone had broken the fourth wall, leaving only three.

"I'm a... a... lumberjack?"

"Not exactly. You are a cumulative effort between the lumberjacks and the angels to create the perfect hybrid with myth and human."

"A science experiment?"

"For the betterment of everyone. Haven't you heard of *Mill's General Happiness Principle*? We screwed you over to save everyone else." The Lumberjack reached into a random crate and tossed you a lime. "Take a bite. The effects of the lime will counteract all of the time you've been in cryostasis."

You took a bite from the citrus and the bones in your legs hardened. In a solid ten seconds, you could finally stand up completely straight. It was possible that fruit was more magical than you had initially thought, but you weren't really sure. Nor did it really matter.

"While the Devil was running her little mind experiment, we were busy creating you. There isn't a you in this you-niverse, so we needed to create one." You looked down, and it was then that you realized you had no belly button.

"So, my life is trivial?" You felt the interior of your mind constrict. Consciousness was sweeping through you, and the sting of breath pushed into your lungs. This is existence. Your mind popped and crackled to life. A pain radiated through your chest. Seconds, if not minutes, ago, you hadn't existed, and you may very well never have existed if the pod had never opened.

"Not unless you're fond of trivia about saving the universe from a transdimensional demon," the lumberjack said.

You felt like you had already learned that lumberjacks were mythical creatures, and that the Devil was after you. A warm tingling sensation overtook your brain, and it felt like warm water was dripping down your ear. The lumberjack took a step closer to you, and clicked your neck back. A disk popped out of your neck. The word *Bland* was written across the front.

"This isn't your disk. We know this disk doesn't work." The lumberjack ripped the disc from your neck and tossed it across the room. You heard it clamber against a far wall and shatter into several pieces.

The lumberjack opened a new CD, and you felt the cool disc press into your neck. It was empty and hollow in comparison. In fact, the music you had been hearing, all but faded away from existence. It was replaced with the slight hum of white noise. The hum drowned out everything you attempted to think.

"Soon, you will be ready to take on the Devil. She won't know what hit her."

From there, the lumberjack was the only person you saw. He forced you to train in the hot sun to simulate the heat of the Devil's wrath. The blazing sun was enough to fry your skin to a deep red. Every night that you tried to sleep, the heat was trapped under your skin until you were angry. Until you were ready to kill the lumberjack.

"What are you trying to do to me? I'm a person!" you screamed.

"You aren't a person. You're a mindless killing machine," the lumberjack said without hesitation.

Without thinking, your anger manifested as fire from your mouth, and you went to bite the lumberjack. He was keen to pull the ax from his belt and swing, luckily he stopped just short of cutting your face off. The resulting strike split your tongue down the center, causing the fire to fall back into your gullet.

"You're lucky," he said, but you really didn't feel like it.

From that day forward, you were locked into the glass dome that you were born from. Without a blanket and without music. You wanted your album back, you wanted everything back. You wanted your bland life back, but it was out of reach. You probably would never get a real life back.

A day later or a year later, whichever, time was

strange to you, the lumberjack woke you up. As you awoke, an alarm filled the cement room you slept in. It was deep red with an acid trumpet sound. You had been briefed over the alarm by him before. It was the alarm that sounded once the Devil made her way to your Z-universe. Your job was to kill her, because that was destined in lumberjack lore. Bright arrows illuminated your path down a cement hallway.

"She should be here soon," the lumberjack screamed from the main room. You slid in there, ready to fight the Devil.

"Where is she?" you screamed.

"Right behind you! Look out!" But when you turned around, nobody was there. You could see your shadow playing against the wall with its edges burned orange.

"She isn't behind me."

You fazed into your shadow, feeling the demonic powers shift through your body. They created you. They thought they needed you, but you were the thing they were supposed to avoid. Your mind was an uncontrollable mess of evil and darkness. The darkness opened to the sunset. As you walked across the rocky bluff you appeared on, you saw the sun and moon close to each other. Again, you could hear a song from **bland.** It was the one that played after the register closed. You contemplated the evil inside of you, wishing that it would fade away, but it was yours. You could choose how to use it or when to use it, but you could never be rid of it.

You walked towards the edge feeling the music shift

back into your ears as you contemplated good and evil. You hummed for a moment and then sang.

"Sold my soul to the Devil for 50 cents." It dawned on you though that the Devil was never going to appear here. She was never destined to make it here. The entire time, you were destined to be her. There were too many firewalls for her to get passed, but that didn't stop something from growing within.

You came to a sudden stop at the edge of the cliff and so did your album. If you were always destined to kill the Devil that implied you were destined to.... Your mind couldn't complete the idea. You stood there, looking towards the sunset and listening the slow violin music seep into your album.

You wondered if the album could be changed. Clearly it could be molded in different ways, but it always snapped back. If it could never be changed, then that meant neither could you. If it could be stretched, maybe you could change. The darkness inside couldn't be all that you were. The sunset continued to set and the album gained a slight crescendo, building towards something new. Once the sun completely set, you knew you would have to make a choice by moonlight, but no matter what happened, you would have your own personal music. It would play in your heart and in your head, because it was yours, and it was the beat that you walked too.

The final glimpse of sunlight flickered away and you heard the quarters again. 50 cents seemed so small sometimes, but it could also bring so much joy to a child. Maybe you sold your soul for joy. Even if you were destined to Hell, you could make the best of what you had. You would have to decide either way, because this was your last choice, but it wasn't the final one.

About the Author

A.M. HOUNCHELL IS a graduate of Washburn University where he studied English. He has several published books under his belt, but should consider buying a new belt and keeping his books on shelves. A.M.  was raised by two loving grandparents, who fostered creativity by always believing in him, even if half the things he said didn't make sense to them. Currently, he lives in Topeka, Kansas with his wife, two cats, and two birds.

Check out A.M. Hounchell's other books on Amazon:

www.amazon.com/A.M.-Hounchell/e/B01LAHL546

A.M. Hounchell's blog:

http://prosefessor.blogspot.com/

Follow A.M. Hounchell on Twitter: @inferno4dante

If You Have Enjoyed this Book,
Please Check Out These Other Titles from the
Catalogue of Rusty Wheels Media, LLC.

Letters Never Meant to be Read (Volume II)

Letters Never Meant to be Read (Volume I)

Worked Stiff: Poetry and Prose for the Common

Worked Stiff: Short Stories to Tell Your Boss

Where Did You Go?:
A 21st Century Guide to Finding Yourself Again

The Forge: Certified Six Sigma Green Belt
Certification Program Workbook

**If you have any submissions of your own, send them
to us. Unique writing and letters will always be
considered for the collection…**
rustywheelsmedia@gmail.com

or

Rusty Wheels Media, LLC
PO Box 1692
Rome, GA 30162

They keep
turning...

www.ingramcontent.com/pod-product-compliance
Lightning Source LLC
Chambersburg PA
CBHW070555180626
46817CB00005B/1843